英語即席演講是可以準備的！

　　一般英語演講比賽，都是先比賽「指定題目」，之後，再比賽「看圖即席演講」。「指定題目」的演講，可以事先準備，只要背熟，就可以勝過別人。但是「看圖即席演講」，一般人認為無法準備，要靠實力。

　　事實上，「看圖即席演講」也是可以事先準備的。本書包含「萬用開場白」及「萬用結尾語」，幾乎什麼比賽題目都可以用得到。另外還有 20 回「即席演講」練習，每篇都是以「一口氣英語」的方式，三句一組，九句一段，每一篇 27 句，剛好 2 分鐘左右；第 16～20 回，每一篇有 54 句，可在 4 分鐘之內講完。

　　背了會忘記，是學英語最大的障礙。好在本書採用「一口氣英語」的方式，讀者如果能將書中的演講稿背熟之後，再加快速度，變成直覺，就終生不會忘記，唯有不忘記，才能累積。碰到新的題目，可以在腦海中，將背過的句子排列組合成新的演講。

　　演講稿中的句子，我們儘量以短句呈現，句子越短，越有力量，說起來就越有信心。想要參加演講比賽，就得一年前開始準備。參加英語演講比賽，是一項挑戰，也是一個學英文的好方法。

　　本書在編審及校對的每一階段，均力求完善，但恐有疏漏之處，誠盼各界先進不吝批評指正。

劉　毅

1. Something interesting happened today.
   It was quite extraordinary.
   I can hardly believe it myself.

2. Do you see the people there?
   Do you know what they are doing?
   Let me explain.

3. Let me tell you about a very surprising event.
   It took the wind out of me.
   I'm still reeling from the shock.

4. Each place has its local customs.
   These people seem to be performing something.
   Let's see what they're up to.

5. There's a large crowd gathered here.
   Let's find out what's up.
   Let's see what all the fuss is about.

6. This is breaking news.
   I am reporting live from the scene.
   You're not going to believe your ears.

7. There's something I feel you must know.
   It's imperative you have this knowledge.
   It can't wait a single moment.

8. Here's a great opportunity.
   Here's a chance to make it big.
   Allow me to explain.

9. Want to learn how to play a game?
   It's not difficult at all.
   I'll tell you how to go about it.

1. I guess it was all for the good.
Regardless, it was definitely memorable.
I'll keep it in my mind always.

2. Now you have a better understanding.
Now you know what's going on.
I hope my explanation clarified things.

3. Experience is the best teacher.
Now I've learned my lesson.
I'll never repeat the same mistake again.

4. Aren't local customs fascinating?
I hope my tour has been entertaining.
I hope you've learned a thing or two.

5. Now isn't that interesting?
Bet you don't see that every day.
I know I sure don't.

6. This is the end of my coverage.
This concludes my report.
Thanks for tuning in.

7. I hope what I told you was helpful.
I hope I've been of service.
There's nothing I like better than helping others out.

8. I've told you all you need to know.
Now it's up to you.
See if you can do it.

9. Doesn't that sound like fun?
Isn't it a neat idea?
Now you can try it.

英語即席演講 ❶

準備時間：2分鐘

演講時間：2分鐘

【資料來源：和平高中高一即席演講比賽】

 Speech 1

This is a picture of a typical family.
It represents the roles parents play.
It shows us how hard mothers work.

Looking at this picture, I think
　of my mom.
I realize how much she did for me.
I really appreciate her so much.

My dad is a kind man.
He was always nice to me.
But my mom did all the tough jobs.

typical〔ˈtɪpɪkl̩〕　　　represent〔ˌrɛprɪˈzɛnt〕
role〔rol〕　　　　　play〔ple〕
show〔ʃo〕　　　　　hard〔hɑrd〕
realize〔ˈriəˌlaɪz〕　　appreciate〔əˈpriʃɪˌet〕
kind〔kaɪnd〕　　　　tough〔tʌf〕

***The lady above is like a magician*.**
She is doing several tasks at the
　　same time.
She is exhausted yet she doesn't quit.

She just got home from her office.
She's taking care of her family.
This lady is a "superwoman."

She's vacuuming the floor.
She's undressing the little boy.
She's trying to let her husband take
　　a rest.

---

lady (ˈledɪ)	above (əˈbʌv)
magician (məˈdʒɪʃən)	task (tæsk)
at the same time	exhausted (ɪgˈzɔstɪd)
yet (jɛt)	quit (kwɪt)
get (gɛt)	*take care of*
superwoman (ˈsupɚˌwʊmən)	
vacuum (ˈvækjuəm)	floor (flor)
undress (ʌnˈdrɛs)	*try to* + *V*.
husband (ˈhʌzbənd)	*take a rest*

I sympathize with her.

The husband should get up and help out.

The husband is being selfish and lazy.

How can he just sit there reading the
  paper?

Look, he's got his feet up.

No wonder people say it's a man's world.

I don't think we can generalize.

I know many men who help cook
  and clean.

My grandpa is the perfect example.

sympathize (ˈsɪmpəˌθaɪz)	***get up***
help out	selfish (ˈsɛlfɪʃ)
lazy (ˈlezɪ)	paper (ˈpepɚ)
no wonder	
generalize (ˈdʒɛnərəlˌaɪz)	cook (kʊk)
clean (klin)	grandpa (ˈgrændpɑ)
perfect (ˈpɝfɪkt)	example (ɪgˈzæmpl̩)

■ Speech 1

● 演講解說

This is a picture of a typical family.	這是一個典型家庭的圖片。
It represents the roles parents play.	它描繪出父母親所扮演的角色。
It shows us how hard mothers work.	它告訴我們母親有多努力工作。
Looking at this picture, I think of my mom.	看著這張圖片，我想到我的媽媽。
I realize how much she did for me.	我知道她為我做的有多少。
I really appreciate her so much.	我真的很欣賞她。
My dad is a kind man.	我爸爸是一個親切的人。
He was always nice to me.	他總是對我很好。
But my mom did all the tough jobs.	但是我媽媽要做所有困難的工作。

＊＊————————————————

typical〔ˈtɪpɪkḷ〕*adj.* 典型的　　represent〔͵rɛprɪˈzɛnt〕*v.* 代表；描繪
role〔rol〕*n.* 角色　　play〔ple〕*v.* 扮演　　show〔ʃo〕*v.* 告訴
hard〔hɑrd〕*adv.* 努力地　　realize〔ˈrɪə͵laɪz〕*v.* 知道；了解
appreciate〔əˈpriʃɪ͵et〕*v.* 欣賞　　kind〔kaɪnd〕*adj.* 親切的
tough〔tʌf〕*adj.* 困難的

The lady above is like a magician.   圖上的女人就像個魔術師。

She is doing several tasks at the same time.   她同時做好幾件工作。

She is exhausted yet she doesn't quit.   她筋疲力竭，但卻沒有停下來。

She just got home from her office.   她才剛下班回家。

She's taking care of her family.   她正在照顧她的家人。

This lady is a "superwoman."   這位女士是「女超人」。

She's vacuuming the floor.   她正在用吸塵器吸地板。

She's undressing the little boy.   她正在脫掉小男孩的衣服。

She's trying to let her husband take a rest.   她想要讓她的丈夫休息一下。

＊＊

lady〔ˈledɪ〕*n.* 女士　　above〔əˈbʌv〕*adv.* 在上方

magician〔məˈdʒɪʃən〕*n.* 魔術師　　task〔tæsk〕*n.* 工作；任務

at the same time 同時　　exhausted〔ɪgˈzɔstɪd〕*adj.* 筋疲力竭的

yet〔jɛt〕*conj.* 但是　　quit〔kwɪt〕*v.* 停止　　get〔gɛt〕*v.* 到達

take care of 照顧　　superwoman〔ˈsupɚˌwumən〕*n.* 女超人

vacuum〔ˈvækjuəm〕*v.* 用吸塵器打掃　　floor〔flor〕*n.* 地板

undress〔ʌnˈdrɛs〕*v.* 脫掉（某人的）衣服

try to + V. 試著～；想要～　　husband〔ˈhʌzbənd〕*n.* 丈夫

take a rest 休息一下

I sympathize with her.	我同情她。
The husband should get up and help out.	那個丈夫應該站起來幫忙。
The husband is being selfish and lazy.	那個丈夫很自私而且懶惰。
How can he just sit there reading the paper?	他怎麼可以就坐在那裡看報紙？
Look, he's got his feet up.	看，他把腳抬起來。
No wonder people say it's a man's world.	難怪人們會說，這是男人的世界。
I don't think we can generalize.	我不認為我們可以概括而論。
I know many men who help cook and clean.	我認識很多會幫忙煮飯及打掃的男人。
My grandpa is the perfect example.	我爺爺就是個完美的例子。

** ——————————————

sympathize〔'sɪmpə,θaɪz〕*v.* 同情　　***get up*** 站起來
help out 幫忙　　selfish〔'sɛlfɪʃ〕*adj.* 自私的
lazy〔'lezɪ〕*adj.* 懶惰的　　paper〔'pepɚ〕*n.* 報紙 (= *newspaper*)
get〔gɛt〕*v.* 使　　***no wonder*** 難怪
generalize〔'dʒɛnərəl,aɪz〕*v.* 概括而論　　cook〔kʊk〕*v.* 煮飯
clean〔klin〕*v.* 打掃　　grandpa〔'grændpɑ〕*n.* 爺爺
perfect〔'pɝfɪkt〕*adj.* 完美的　　example〔ɪg'zæmpl̩〕*n.* 例子

英語即席演講 ❷

準備時間：2 分鐘

演講時間：2 分鐘

【資料來源：華江高中即席演講比賽】

Speech 2

Ted and Ken witnessed a crime.
A robber broke a glass window.
He attempted to rob the candy store.

Ted and Ken were not afraid.
They startled the thief.
They caught him red-handed.

The robber decided to run for it.
They could not let him get away.
They hoped to bring him to justice.

witness ('wɪtnɪs)	crime (kraɪm)
robber ('rɑbɚ)	break (brek)
glass (glæs)	attempt (ə'tɛmpt)
rob (rɑb)	candy ('kændɪ)
afraid (ə'fred)	startle ('stɑrtl̩)
thief (θif)	red-handed ('rɛd'hændɪd)
catch sb. red-handed	decide (dɪ'saɪd)
run for it	*get away*
justice ('dʒʌstɪs)	*bring sb. to justice*

The robber tried to escape.

He darted off.

He looked nervously behind him.

Ted and Ken ran like the wind.

They were gaining on him.

They were intent on catching him.

They tackled the criminal.

They jumped on him and beat him up.

The criminal was finally caught.

try to + ***V.***	escape ﹝ ə'skep ﹞
dart ﹝ dɑrt ﹞	***dart off***
nervously ﹝'nɝvəslɪ ﹞	wind ﹝ wɪnd ﹞
like the wind	***gain on***
intent ﹝ ɪn'tɛnt ﹞	***be intent on***
tackle ﹝'tækḷ ﹞	criminal ﹝'krɪmənḷ ﹞
jump ﹝ dʒʌmp ﹞	***jump on***
beat up	finally ﹝'faɪnḷɪ ﹞

The director yelled, ***"Cut!"***
It had all just been an act!
It had been a film in the making.

Ted and Ken had disrupted the filming.
The thief was in fact just an actor.
The kids had made a big mistake.

The director was fuming over the
   interference.
The kids weren't to blame, however.
The actor had acted too well!

---

director (də'rɛktɚ)

cut (kʌt)

film (fɪlm)

disrupt (dɪs'rʌpt)

actor ('æktɚ)

fume (fjum)

interference (,ɪntɚ'fɪrəns)

be to blame

yell (jɛl)

act (ækt)

in the making

in fact

make a mistake

fume over *sth.*

blame (blem)

however (haʊ'ɛvɚ)

■ Speech 2

● 演講解說

Ted and Ken witnessed a crime.	泰德和肯目睹一椿犯罪事件。
A robber broke a glass window.	有個搶匪打破玻璃窗。
He attempted to rob the candy store.	他企圖搶劫糖果店。
Ted and Ken were not afraid.	泰德和肯並不害怕。
They startled the thief.	他們讓小偷嚇一跳。
They caught him red-handed.	他們當場逮到他犯罪。
The robber decided to run for it.	那名搶匪決定趕快逃跑。
They could not let him get away.	他們不能讓他逃走。
They hoped to bring him to justice.	他們希望能將他移送法辦。

** ────────────────

witness〔ˈwɪtnɪs〕 *v.* 目擊;看見　　crime〔kraɪm〕 *n.* 犯罪

robber〔ˈrɑbɚ〕 *n.* 搶匪;強盜　　break〔brek〕 *v.* 打破

glass〔glæs〕 *adj.* 玻璃的　　attempt〔əˈtɛmpt〕 *v.* 企圖

rob〔rɑb〕 *v.* 搶劫　　candy〔ˈkændɪ〕 *n.* 糖果

afraid〔əˈfred〕 *adj.* 害怕的　　startle〔ˈstɑrtl̩〕 *v.* 使嚇一跳

thief〔θif〕 *n.* 小偷;賊　　red-handed〔ˈrɛdˈhændɪd〕 *adj.* 現行犯的

catch *sb.* ***red-handed*** 當場發現某人的罪行

decide〔dɪˈsaɪd〕 *v.* 決定　　***run for it*** 快跑

get away 逃離　　justice〔ˈdʒʌstɪs〕 *n.* 司法;審判

bring *sb.* ***to justice*** 將某人移送法辦;審判某人

The robber tried to escape.	搶匪試著逃跑。
He darted off.	他飛奔而逃。
He looked nervously behind him.	他很緊張地往後看。
Ted and Ken ran like the wind.	泰德和肯飛快地跑著。
They were gaining on him.	他們快要趕上他了。
They were intent on catching him.	他們一心想要抓住他。
They tackled the criminal.	他們抓住了罪犯。
They jumped on him and beat him up.	他們突然撲向他，把他痛打一頓。
The criminal was finally caught.	罪犯終於被抓住了。

**

try to + V. 試著～；想要～　　escape〔əˋskep〕*v.* 逃走
dart〔dɑrt〕*v.* 狂奔　　*dart off* 飛奔而去
nervously〔ˋnɝvəslɪ〕*adv.* 緊張地　　wind〔wɪnd〕*n.* 風
like the wind 飛快地　　*gain on* 趕上
intent〔ɪnˋtɛnt〕*adj.* 專心的　　*be intent on* 專心於…的
tackle〔ˋtækḷ〕*v.* 抓住　　criminal〔ˋkrɪmənḷ〕*n.* 罪犯
jump〔dʒʌmp〕*v.* 跳　　*jump on* 突然撲向；突然攻擊
beat up 痛打　　finally〔ˋfaɪnḷɪ〕*adv.* 最後；終於

The director yelled, *"Cut!"* 　　　　　　導演大喊：「卡！」

It had all just been an act! 　　　　　　這全都是在演戲！

It had been a film in the making. 　　　　這是在拍片。

Ted and Ken had disrupted the 　　　　　泰德和肯打斷了影片的拍攝。
　　filming.

The thief was in fact just an actor. 　　　那個小偷事實上只是個演員。

The kids had made a big mistake. 　　　　這兩個孩子犯了大錯。

The director was fuming over 　　　　　　導演因爲他們的擾亂而發怒。
　　the interference.

The kids weren't to blame, however. 　　可是這兩個孩子不該被責備。

The actor had acted too well! 　　　　　那個演員演得太好了！

** ──────────────────

director〔dəˈrɛktɚ〕*n.* 導演　　yell〔jɛl〕*v.* 吼叫；大喊

cut〔kʌt〕*v.* 停止拍攝　　act〔ækt〕*n.* (戲劇的) 一幕　*v.* 表演；演出

film〔fɪlm〕*n.* 影片　*v.* 拍攝影片　　*in the making* 在製造中

disrupt〔dɪsˈrʌpt〕*v.* 使中斷　　*in fact* 事實上

actor〔ˈæktɚ〕*n.* 演員　　*make a mistake* 犯錯

fume〔fjum〕*v.* 發怒　　*fume over sth.* 爲某事發怒

interference〔ˌɪntɚˈfɪrəns〕*n.* 擾亂　　blame〔blem〕*v.* 責備

be to blame 該受責備　　however〔hauˈɛvɚ〕*adv.* 然而；可是

英語即席演講❸

準備時間：2 分鐘

演講時間：2 分鐘

【資料來源：華江高中即席演講比賽】

Speech 3

A car has had a flat in the road.
It is now rush hour.
It is the time when traffic is craziest.

The driver is changing his tire.
He is trying to fix the situation.
He is under a lot of stress.

He has created a traffic jam.
He is the object of everyone's anger.
Even the police officer is glaring at him.

flat〔flæt〕

traffic〔'træfɪk〕

change〔tʃendʒ〕

fix〔fɪks〕

stress〔strɛs〕

a traffic jam

anger〔'æŋgɚ〕

glare〔glɛr〕

rush hour

crazy〔'krezɪ〕

tire〔taɪr〕

situation〔͵sɪtʃu'eʃən〕

create〔krɪ'et〕

object〔'ɑbdʒɪkt〕

police officer

Someone should offer him some help.

Someone should lend him a hand.

It is useless to yell at the poor man.

Give him assistance.

Call a tow truck for him.

The traffic jam would disappear more
   quickly.

Any form of aid would be appreciated.

It would save everyone a lot of time.

Blaming the man only increases tension.

---

offer ('ɔfɚ)

useless ('juslɪs)

poor (pʊr)

tow truck

form (fɔrm)

appreciate (ə'priʃɪ,et)

blame (blem)

tension ('tɛnʃən)

lend *sb.* ***a hand***

yell (jɛl)

assistance (ə'sɪstəns)

disappear (,dɪsə'pɪr)

aid (ed)

save (sev)

increase (ɪn'kris)

***Courtesy on the road is important*.**

Put away your resentment and be polite.

Put-downs will only cause conflict.

Many drivers tend to be too impatient.

Patience is a virtue.

Lack of it causes distress.

We all encounter car trouble sometimes.

We should put ourselves in others' shoes.

Let's make the road a friendlier place.

---

courtesy〔'kɝtəsɪ〕	important〔ɪm'pɔrtn̩t〕
put away	resentment〔rɪ'zɛntmənt〕
polite〔pə'laɪt〕	put-down〔'pʊt,daʊn〕
cause〔kɔz〕	conflict〔'kɑnflɪkt〕
***tend to + V*.**	impatient〔ɪm'peʃənt〕
patience〔'peʃəns〕	virtue〔'vɝtʃʊ〕
lack〔læk〕	distress〔dɪ'strɛs〕
encounter〔ɪn'kaʊntɚ〕	trouble〔'trʌbl̩〕
put oneself in sb.'s shoes	friendly〔'frɛndlɪ〕

■ Speech 3

● 演講解說

A car has had a flat in the road.	路上有輛車爆胎。
It is now rush hour.	現在是尖峰時間。
It is the time when traffic is craziest.	現在是交通最混亂的時間。
The driver is changing his tire.	那位駕駛人正在換輪胎。
He is trying to fix the situation.	他試著要解決這個情況。
He is under a lot of stress.	他承受很大的壓力。
He has created a traffic jam.	他造成塞車。
He is the object of everyone's anger.	他是大家生氣的對象。
Even the police officer is glaring at him.	甚至連警察都瞪著他。

**

flat〔flæt〕*n.* 洩氣的輪胎   *rush hour* 尖峰時間

traffic〔'træfɪk〕*n.* 交通   crazy〔'krezɪ〕*adj.* 瘋狂的

change〔tʃendʒ〕*v.* 更換   tire〔taɪr〕*n.* 輪胎   fix〔fɪks〕*v.* 解決

situation〔͵sɪtʃu'eʃən〕*n.* 情況   stress〔strɛs〕*n.* 壓力

create〔krɪ'et〕*v.* 引起;造成   *a traffic jam* 交通阻塞

object〔'ɑbdʒɪkt〕*n.* 對象   anger〔'æŋgɚ〕*n.* 生氣

police officer 警察   glare〔glɛr〕*v.* 瞪著 < *at* >

Someone should offer him some help.　應該有人來幫助他。

Someone should lend him a hand.　應該有人向他伸出援手。

It is useless to yell at the poor　對這個可憐的男人大叫是沒

　man.　用的。

Give him assistance.　要幫助他。

Call a tow truck for him.　替他叫拖吊車。

The traffic jam would disappear　交通阻塞會更快消失。

　more quickly.

Any form of aid would be　任何形式的幫助都會讓他很

　appreciated.　感激。

It would save everyone a lot of time.　這樣會節省大家很多時間。

Blaming the man only increases　責備那個男人只會使情勢更

　tension.　緊張。

**

offer 〔'ɔfɚ〕 *v.* 提供;給予　　*lend sb. a hand* 幫助某人

useless 〔'juslɪs〕 *adj.* 無用的　　yell 〔jɛl〕 *v.* 大叫

poor 〔pur〕 *adj.* 可憐的　　assistance 〔ə'sɪstəns〕 *n.* 幫助

tow truck 拖吊車　　disappear 〔ˌdɪsə'pɪr〕 *v.* 消失

form 〔fɔrm〕 *n.* 形式　　aid 〔ed〕 *n.* 幫助

appreciate 〔ə'priʃɪˌet〕 *v.* 感激　　save 〔sev〕 *v.* 節省

blame 〔blem〕 *v.* 責備　　increase 〔ɪn'kris〕 *v.* 增加

tension 〔'tɛnʃən〕 *n.* (情勢的) 緊張

Courtesy on the road is important.	道路禮儀很重要。
Put away your resentment and be polite.	拋開你的憤怒，有禮貌一點。
Put-downs will only cause conflict.	令人難堪的話只會造成衝突。
Many drivers tend to be too impatient.	許多駕駛人都很容易不耐煩。
Patience is a virtue.	耐心是一種美德。
Lack of it causes distress.	缺乏耐心會使人苦惱。
We all encounter car trouble sometimes.	我們有時都會碰到車子故障的情況。
We should put ourselves in other's shoes.	我們應該站在別人的立場想。
Let's make the road a friendlier place.	讓我們把道路變成更友善的地方吧。

** ─────────────────────

courtesy〔'kɝtəsɪ〕*n.* 禮儀   important〔ɪm'pɔrtṇt〕*adj.* 重要的
put away 收拾；放棄；摒棄   resentment〔rɪ'zɛntmənt〕*n.* 氣憤
polite〔pə'laɪt〕*adj.* 有禮貌的
put-down〔'pʊt,daʊn〕*n.* 令人難堪的言語或行為   cause〔kɔz〕*v.* 造成
conflict〔'kɑnflɪkt〕*n.* 衝突   ***tend to + V.*** 易於～
impatient〔ɪm'peʃənt〕*adj.* 不耐煩的   patience〔'peʃəns〕*n.* 耐心
virtue〔'vɝtʃu〕*n.* 美德   lack〔læk〕*n.* 缺乏
distress〔dɪ'strɛs〕*n.* 苦惱；痛苦   encounter〔ɪn'kaʊntɚ〕*v.* 遭遇
trouble〔'trʌbḷ〕*n.* 故障   ***put oneself in sb.'s shoes*** 站在某人的立場想
friendly〔'frɛndlɪ〕*adj.* 友善的

英語即席演講 ❹

準備時間：2分鐘

演講時間：2分鐘

【資料來源：和平高中高二即席演講比賽】

Speech 4

Many children are visiting the zoo.
They are disturbing the animals.
They are breaking the rules.

The tiger is upset by a girl's tapping.
The elephant may get ill when fed scraps.
The kids are causing the animals discomfort.

Animals need peace and quiet.
Let's admire them from a distance.
Let's not forget the rules of the zoo.

visit ('vɪzɪt)   disturb (dɪ'stɝb)
break (brek)   rule (rul)
upset (ʌp'sɛt)   tap (tæp)
feed (fid)   scraps (skræps)
cause (kɔz)   discomfort (dɪs'kʌmfɚt)
peace (pis)   quiet ('kwaɪət)
peace and quiet   admire (əd'maɪr)
distance ('dɪstəns)   forget (fɚ'gɛt)

The rules are for protection.

They protect the animals from harm.

They are also set for our own safety.

We should not violate the rules.

The beasts might get angry and violent.

Someone could be injured.

These rules are set out of respect for life.

These rules are for the welfare of man

and beast.

Follow them; don't break them.

protection (prə'tɛkʃən)   protect (prə'tɛkt)

harm (harm)   set (sɛt)

safety ('sefti)   violate ('vaɪə,let)

beast (bist)   violent ('vaɪələnt)

injure ('ɪndʒə)   ***out of***

respect (rɪ'spɛkt)   welfare ('wɛl,fɛr)

man (mæn)   follow ('falo)

Obeying rules is important everywhere.

Especially in public places.

Especially when it involves safety.

Rules are for the benefit of everyone.

Rules keep order in our society.

Rules prevent people from harming
    others.

Regulations are there for a reason.

Neglecting them may be disastrous.

Behave well and follow the rules!

obey (o'be)	important (ɪm'pɔrtn̩t)
everywhere ('ɛvrɪ,hwɛr)	especially (ə'spɛʃəlɪ)
public ('pʌblɪk)	involve (ɪn'vɑlv)
benefit ('bɛnəfɪt)	keep (kip)
order ('ɔrdɚ)	society (sə'saɪətɪ)
prevent (prɪ'vɛnt)	regulation (,rɛgjə'leʃən)
reason ('rizn̩)	neglect (nɪ'glɛkt)
disastrous (dɪz'æstrəs)	behave (bɪ'hev)

■ Speech 4

● 演講解說

Many children are visiting the zoo.	許多孩子正在參觀動物園。
They are disturbing the animals.	他們正在打擾動物。
They are breaking the rules.	他們正在違反規定。
The tiger is upset by a girl's tapping.	有個女孩的拍打讓老虎不高興。
The elephant may get ill when fed scraps.	大象可能會因為被餵食剩餘的食物而生病。
The kids are causing the animals discomfort.	這些孩子正造成動物的不安。
Animals need peace and quiet.	動物需要安靜。
Let's admire them from a distance.	我們從遠處欣賞牠們吧。
Let's not forget the rules of the zoo.	我們不要忘了動物園的規定。

** ─────────────────

visit〔'vɪzɪt〕*v.* 參觀　　disturb〔dɪ'stɝb〕*v.* 打擾
break〔brek〕*v.* 違反　　rule〔rul〕*n.* 規定
upset〔ʌp'sɛt〕*adj.* 不高興的　　tap〔tæp〕*v.* 輕敲；拍打
feed〔fid〕*v.* 餵食【三態變化為：feed-fed〔fɛd〕-fed】
scraps〔skræps〕*n. pl.* 剩餘的食物　　cause〔kɔz〕*v.* (給⋯)帶來
discomfort〔dɪs'kʌmfɚt〕*n.* 不安；不快
peace〔pis〕*n.* 寂靜　　quiet〔'kwaɪət〕*n.* 寂靜；平靜
peace and quiet 安靜　　admire〔əd'maɪr〕*v.* 欣賞
distance〔'dɪstəns〕*n.* 相當的距離；遠處　　forget〔fɚ'gɛt〕*v.* 忘記

The rules are for protection.	規定是爲了要保護。
They protect the animals from harm.	它們保護動物不受傷害。
They are also set for our own safety.	它們也是爲了我們的自身安全而制定。
We should not violate the rules.	我們不該違反規定。
The beasts might get angry and violent.	動物可能會生氣並且變得很兇暴。
Someone could be injured.	可能有人會受傷。
These rules are set out of respect for life.	這些規定是爲了尊重生命而制定。
These rules are for the welfare of man and beast.	這些規定是爲了保障人類和動物的福祉。
Follow them; don't break them.	遵守規定；不要違反規定。

** ——————————————————

protection〔prəˈtɛkʃən〕*n.* 保護   protect〔prəˈtɛkt〕*v.* 保護
harm〔hɑrm〕*n. v.* 傷害   set〔sɛt〕*v.* 制定
safety〔ˈsɛftɪ〕*n.* 安全   violate〔ˈvaɪəˌlet〕*v.* 違反
beast〔bist〕*n.* 動物；野獸
violent〔ˈvaɪələnt〕*adj.* 暴力的；兇暴的
injure〔ˈɪndʒɚ〕*v.* 傷害   ***out of*** 爲了
respect〔rɪˈspɛkt〕*n.* 尊重   welfare〔ˈwɛlˌfɛr〕*n.* 福祉
man〔mæn〕*n.* 人類   follow〔ˈfɑlo〕*v.* 遵守

Obeying rules is important
everywhere.
Especially in public places.
Especially when it involves safety.

不管到哪裡，遵守規定都是
很重要的。
特別是在公共場所。
特別是牽涉到安全時。

Rules are for the benefit of
everyone.
Rules keep order in our society.
Rules prevent people from
harming others.

規定是爲了大家的利益而
制定。
規定能維持我們社會的秩序。
規定能防止人們傷害他人。

Regulations are there for a reason.
Neglecting them may be disastrous.
Behave well and follow the rules!

規定的存在是有原因的。
忽視規定可能會帶來災害。
要表現良好，並遵守規定！

** ——————————————————

obey〔o'be〕*v.* 遵守　　important〔ɪm'pɔrtn̩t〕*adj.* 重要的
everywhere〔'ɛvrɪ,hwɛr〕*adv.* 無論何處
especially〔ə'spɛʃəlɪ〕*adv.* 尤其　　public〔'pʌblɪk〕*adj.* 公共的
involve〔ɪn'vɑlv〕*v.* 牽涉　　benefit〔'bɛnəfɪt〕*n.* 利益；好處
keep〔kip〕*v.* 維持　　order〔'ɔrdɚ〕*n.* 秩序
society〔sə'saɪətɪ〕*n.* 社會　　prevent〔prɪ'vɛnt〕*v.* 防止
regulation〔,rɛgjə'leʃən〕*n.* 規定　　reason〔'rizn̩〕*n.* 理由
neglect〔nɪ'glɛkt〕*v.* 忽視
disastrous〔dɪz'æstrəs〕*adj.* 帶來災害的
behave〔bɪ'hev〕*v.* 行爲；表現

英語即席演講❺

準備時間：2 分鐘

演講時間：2 分鐘

【資料來源：中山女中即席演講比賽】

Speech 5

A child has been abducted.
He is alone and afraid.
He is a victim of a crime.

The boy is blindfolded and frightened.
He is here against his will.
He wonders if he will get out alive.

The kidnapper is nowhere to be seen.
He is probably out collecting ransom.
The boy must try to call for help.

abduct〔æb'dʌkt〕   alone〔ə'lon〕
victim〔'vɪktɪm〕   crime〔kraɪm〕
blindfold〔'blaɪnd,fold〕   frightened〔'fraɪtn̩d〕
will〔wɪl〕   *against* one's *will*
wonder〔'wʌndɚ〕   *get out*
alive〔ə'laɪv〕   kidnapper〔'kɪdnæpɚ〕
nowhere〔'no,hwɛr〕   collect〔kə'lɛkt〕
ransom〔'rænsəm〕   *call for help*

The boy needs to calm down.

He needs to take action.

He needs to find a way out.

He must try to contact someone.

He must help the police locate him.

He must escape from the room.

He should gather his wits.

He should act before it's too late.

There's no telling what the villain

   has in mind.

---

calm (kɑm)	***calm down***
take action	***way out***
contact ('kɑntækt)	police (pə'lis)
locate (lo'ket)	escape (ə'skep)
gather ('gæðɚ)	wits (wɪts)
gather *one's **wits***	act (ækt)
tell (tɛl)	***There is no telling*** ~
what sb. ***has in mind***	villain ('vɪlən)

Actually, *we can avoid being kidnapped*.

Try not to wander off alone.

Try not to go to unfamiliar places.

Let people know where you're going.

Inform someone of your destination.

Tell others when you expect to return.

Be cautious of strangers.

Beware of people you don't know.

Don't become a victim of abduction.

actually (ˈæktʃʊəlɪ)	avoid (əˈvɔɪd)
kidnap (ˈkɪdnæp)	wander (ˈwɑndɚ)
wander off	unfamiliar (ˌʌnfəˈmɪljɚ)
inform (ɪnˈfɔrm)	*inform sb. of sth.*
destination (ˌdɛstəˈneʃən)	expect (ɪkˈspɛkt)
cautious (ˈkɔʃəs)	*be cautious of*
stranger (ˈstrendʒɚ)	beware (bɪˈwɛr)
beware of	abduction (æbˈdʌkʃən)

■ Speech 5

● 演講解說

A child has been abducted.	有個孩子被綁架了。
He is alone and afraid.	他既孤單又害怕。
He is a victim of a crime.	他是犯罪事件的受害者。
The boy is blindfolded and frightened.	他被蒙住眼睛,而且很害怕。
He is here against his will.	他不是自願到這裡來的。
He wonders if he will get out alive.	他不知道自己是否能活著逃出去。
The kidnapper is nowhere to be seen.	綁匪不見蹤影。
He is probably out collecting ransom.	他可能出去拿贖金了。
The boy must try to call for help.	那個男孩必須試著呼救。

** ——————————————————

abduct〔æb'dʌkt〕*v.* 綁架   alone〔ə'lon〕*adj.* 獨自的   *adv.* 獨自地

victim〔'vɪktɪm〕*n.* 受害者   crime〔kraɪm〕*n.* 犯罪

blindfold〔'blaɪnd͵fold〕*v.* 蒙住眼睛   frightened〔'fraɪtn̩d〕*adj.* 害怕的

will〔wɪl〕*n.* 意願   *against one's will* 非出於自願地

wonder〔'wʌndɚ〕*v.* 想知道;不知道(是否)   *get out* 逃脫

alive〔ə'laɪv〕*adj.* 活的   kidnapper〔'kɪdnæpɚ〕*n.* 綁匪

nowhere〔'no͵hwɛr〕*adv.* 什麼地方都沒有   collect〔kə'lɛkt〕*v.* 取回

ransom〔'rænsəm〕*n.* 贖金   *call for help* 呼救

The boy needs to calm down.　　　　　　這個男孩必須冷靜下來。

He needs to take action.　　　　　　　他必須採取行動。

He needs to find a way out.　　　　　　他必須找到出路。

He must try to contact someone.　　　　他必須試著和某個人聯絡。

He must help the police locate him.　　他必須幫助警察找到他。

He must escape from the room.　　　　他必須逃離這個房間。

He should gather his wits.　　　　　　他應該要聚精會神。

He should act before it's too late.　　他應該在為時已晚以前行動。

There's no telling what the villain 　　我們無法得知那個歹徒在想
　　has in mind.　　　　　　　　　　　什麼。

**

calm〔kɑm〕*v.* 冷靜　　*calm down* 冷靜下來

take action 採取行動　　*way out* 擺脫困境的方法；出路

contact〔'kɑntækt〕*v.* 聯絡　　police〔pə'lis〕*n.* 警方

locate〔lo'ket〕*v.* 找出…的位置　　escape〔ə'skep〕*v.* 逃離

gather〔'gæðɚ〕*v.* 集中　　wits〔wɪts〕*n. pl.* 精神

gather one's wits 聚精會神　　act〔ækt〕*v.* 行動

tell〔tɛl〕*v.* 看出；知道

There is no telling ~　無法知道~；難以預料~
　　(= *It is impossible to tell* ~)

what sb. has in mind 某人在想什麼

villain〔'vɪlən〕*n.* 壞蛋；歹徒

***Actually**, we can avoid being kidnapped*.	事實上，我們可以避免被綁架。
Try not to wander off alone.	試著不要獨自一人走散。
Try not to go to unfamiliar places.	試著不要到不熟悉的地方去。
Let people know where you're going.	讓別人知道你要去哪裡。
Inform someone of your destination.	把你的目的地告訴某個人。
Tell others when you expect to return.	告訴別人你預計何時回來。
Be cautious of strangers.	要小心陌生人。
Beware of people you don't know.	要提防你不認識的人。
Don't become a victim of abduction.	不要變成綁架事件的受害者。

** ─────────────

actually〔'æktʃʊəlɪ〕*adv.* 事實上

avoid〔ə'vɔɪd〕*v.* 避免   kidnap〔'kɪdnæp〕*v.* 綁架

wander〔'wɑndɚ〕*v.* 徘徊；迷路   ***wander off*** 與同伴走散；走失

unfamiliar〔͵ʌnfə'mɪljɚ〕*adj.* 不熟悉的

inform〔ɪn'fɔrm〕*v.* 通知；告知

inform *sb. **of** sth.* 通知某人某事

destination〔͵dɛstə'neʃən〕*n.* 目的地   expect〔ɪk'spɛkt〕*v.* 預計

cautious〔'kɔʃəs〕*adj.* 小心的   ***be cautious of*** 小心

stranger〔'strendʒɚ〕*n.* 陌生人   beware〔bɪ'wɛr〕*v.* 小心；提防

beware of 提防   abduction〔æb'dʌkʃən〕*n.* 綁架

英語即席演講 ❻

準備時間：2 分鐘

演講時間：2 分鐘

【資料來源：社會時事考題】

Speech 6

In this picture we see a young lady.

She is busy shopping on the Internet.

She seems very engrossed in it.

This reminds me of my friend Sarah.

She loves to buy things online.

She shops for many hours at a time.

She used to spend her time studying.

Now all she does is shop, shop, shop.

Now she is nearly broke.

---

be busy + V-ing

Internet ('ɪntɚ͵nɛt)

engrossed (ɪn'grost)

Sarah ('sɛrə)

at a time

all one does is + V.

broke (brok)

shop (ʃɑp)

seem (sim)

remind (rɪ'maɪnd)

online ('ɑn͵laɪn)

used to

nearly ('nɪrlɪ)

Sarah is wasting time and money.

She is falling behind in school.

She is spending all her savings.

She clicks the mouse all day long.

She has forgotten the more important
    things in life.

For example: family, health,
    and education.

As her friend, I am quite worried.

I tried to talk some sense into her.

I tried to help her out.

waste〔west〕	***fall behind***
savings〔'sevɪŋz〕	click〔klɪk〕
mouse〔maʊs〕	***all day long***
important〔ɪm'pɔrtn̩t〕	***for example***
health〔hɛlθ〕	education〔ˌɛdʒə'keʃən〕
quite〔kwaɪt〕	sense〔sɛns〕
talk some sense into sb.	***help sb. out***

We should not lose control of ourselves.

Online shopping is convenient.

But it could be trouble in disguise.

Many items are not necessary.

We do not need to buy them.

We could get into debt if we do.

We should spend our money wisely.

We should use our time properly.

The Internet should be our friend,

   not our enemy.

control〔kənˈtrol〕

convenient〔kənˈvinjənt〕

disguise〔dɪsˈgaɪz〕

trouble in disguise

necessary〔ˈnɛsəˌsɛrɪ〕

get into debt

properly〔ˈprɑpɚlɪ〕

trouble〔ˈtrʌbl̩〕

in disguise

item〔ˈaɪtəm〕

debt〔dɛt〕

wisely〔ˈwaɪzlɪ〕

enemy〔ˈɛnəmɪ〕

■ Speech 6

● 演講解說

In this picture we see a young lady.	我們在這張圖裡看到一個年輕女子。
She is busy shopping on the Internet.	她正忙著在網路上購物。
She seems very engrossed in it.	她似乎非常熱衷。
This reminds me of my friend Sarah.	這使我想起我的朋友莎拉。
She loves to buy things online.	她很喜歡上網買東西。
She shops for many hours at a time.	她一次要買好幾個小時。
She used to spend her time studying.	她以前常花時間讀書。
Now all she does is shop, shop, shop.	現在她只是不停地買。
Now she is nearly broke.	現在她快要破產了。

＊＊ ─────────────────

be busy* + *V-ing 忙於～　　shop〔ʃɑp〕*v.* 購物
Internet〔'ɪntɚ‚nɛt〕*n.* 網際網路　　seem〔sim〕*v.* 似乎
engrossed〔ɪn'grost〕*adj.* 熱衷的；著迷的
remind〔rɪ'maɪnd〕*v.* 使想起　　Sarah〔'sɛrə〕*n.*【女子名】莎拉
online〔'ɑn‚laɪn〕*adv.* 在網路上　*adj.* 網路上的　***at a time*** 一次
used to 以前　　***all one does is* + *V.*** 某人所做的就只是～
nearly〔'nɪrlɪ〕*adv.* 幾乎　　broke〔brok〕*adj.* 破產的；沒錢的

Sarah is wasting time and money.	莎拉在浪費時間和金錢。
She is falling behind in school.	她在學校的功課落後。
She is spending all her savings.	她快花光她所有的積蓄。
She clicks the mouse all day long.	她一整天都在按滑鼠。
She has forgotten the more important things in life.	她忘了人生中更重要的事。
For example: family, health, and education.	例如：家庭、健康和教育。
As her friend, I am quite worried.	身為她的朋友，我相當擔心。
I tried to talk some sense into her.	我試著要和她講道理。
I tried to help her out.	我試著要幫助她。

**

waste〔west〕*v.* 浪費   *fall behind* 落後

savings〔'sevɪŋz〕*n. pl.* 儲蓄

click〔klɪk〕*v.* 發出喀嗒聲；按（滑鼠）

mouse〔maʊs〕*n.* 滑鼠   *all day long* 整天

important〔ɪm'pɔrtn̩t〕*adj.* 重要的   *for example* 例如

health〔hɛlθ〕*n.* 健康   education〔ˌɛdʒə'keʃən〕*n.* 教育

quite〔kwaɪt〕*adv.* 相當   sense〔sɛns〕*n.* 道理

talk some sense into sb. 與某人講道理

help sb. out 幫助某人

We should not lose control of

   ourselves.

我們不應該失控。

Online shopping is convenient.

在網路上購物很方便。

But it could be trouble in disguise.

但卻可能隱藏著麻煩。

Many items are not necessary.

許多東西都不是必需品。

We do not need to buy them.

我們不需要買那些東西。

We could get into debt if we do.

如果我們買了，可能就會負債。

We should spend our money wisely.

我們應該聰明地花錢。

We should use our time properly.

我們應該適當地運用時間。

The Internet should be our friend,

網路應該是我們的朋友，

   not our enemy.

而不是敵人。

** ─────────────

control〔kən'trol〕*n.* 控制

convenient〔kən'vinjənt〕*adj.* 方便的

trouble〔'trʌbl̩〕*n.* 麻煩

disguise〔dɪs'ɡaɪz〕*n.* 偽裝　　*in disguise* 偽裝的

trouble in disguise 偽裝的麻煩【在此指「隱藏的麻煩」】

item〔'aɪtəm〕*n.* 物品　　necessary〔'nɛsəˏsɛrɪ〕*adj.* 必需的

debt〔dɛt〕*n.* 負債（的狀態）　　*get into debt* 負債；欠債

wisely〔'waɪzlɪ〕*adv.* 聰明地

properly〔'prɑpəˏlɪ〕*adv.* 適當地　　enemy〔'ɛnəmɪ〕*n.* 敵人

英語即席演講 ❼

準備時間：2分鐘

演講時間：2分鐘

【資料來源：社會時事考題】

Speech 7

A traveler visits a market in India.
Through his eyes we see poverty.
Through India we see a world in need.

The streets are filled with trash.
It is not a healthy environment.
It needs to be cleaned up.

A boy is begging for money.
He is hungry and homeless.
How desperate he must feel.

traveler〔ˈtrævlɚ〕	market〔ˈmɑrkɪt〕
India〔ˈɪndɪə〕	through〔θru〕
poverty〔ˈpɑvɚtɪ〕	need〔nid〕
in need	*be filled with*
trash〔træʃ〕	healthy〔ˈhɛlθɪ〕
environment〔ɪnˈvaɪrənmənt〕	
clean up	beg〔bɛg〕
homeless〔ˈhomlɪs〕	desperate〔ˈdɛspərɪt〕

Poverty is an issue in parts of the world.

Many people don't have anything

　　to eat.

Many can't even find a place to sleep.

Children long to go to school.

It is a farfetched dream to them.

It is a luxury they can't afford.

Without education they can't improve.

They aren't able to care for themselves.

They become a burden to the

　　government.

---

issue (ˈɪʃju)	***long to*** + ***V.***
farfetched (ˈfɑrˈfɛtʃt)	luxury (ˈlʌkʃərɪ)
afford (əˈfɔrd)	improve (ɪmˈpruv)
be able to	***care for***
burden (ˈbɝdn̩)	
government (ˈgʌvə·nmənt)	

I feel very fortunate compared to them.

I never worry about food or money.

I am provided with a good education.

I sympathize with the kids in India.

I want to pitch in to help them someday.

I want to offer them some relief.

Our country may not be the best.

But most of us live quite comfortably.

We are given the chance to pursue

    our dreams!

---

fortunate (ˈfɔrtʃənɪt)   compare (kəmˈpɛr)

compared to   provide (prəˈvaɪd)

sympathize (ˈsɪmpəˌθaɪz)

pitch in   someday (ˈsʌmˌde)

offer (ˈɔfɚ)   relief (rɪˈlif)

comfortably (ˈkʌmfɚtəblɪ)

pursue (pɚˈsu)

■ Speech 7

● 演講解說

A traveler visits a market in India.	有個旅客去逛印度的市場。
Through his eyes we see poverty.	透過他的眼睛，我們看到貧窮。
Through India we see a world in need.	透過印度，我們看到窮困的世界。
The streets are filled with trash.	街上充滿了垃圾。
It is not a healthy environment.	那不是個健康的環境。
It needs to be cleaned up.	那裡需要打掃乾淨。
A boy is begging for money.	有個男孩在乞討錢。
He is hungry and homeless.	他很餓而且無家可歸。
How desperate he must feel.	他一定覺得很絕望。

**

traveler〔'trævlə〕*n.* 旅行者；旅客　　market〔'markɪt〕*n.* 市場
India〔'ɪndɪə〕*n.* 印度　　through〔θru〕*prep.* 透過
poverty〔'pɑvətɪ〕*n.* 貧窮　　need〔nid〕*n.* 窮困；貧窮
in need 窮困中的　　*be filled with* 充滿了
trash〔træʃ〕*n.* 垃圾　　healthy〔'hɛlθɪ〕*adj.* 健康的
environment〔ɪn'vaɪrənmənt〕*n.* 環境　　*clean up* 打掃乾淨
beg〔bɛg〕*v.* 乞求　　homeless〔'homlɪs〕*adj.* 無家可歸的
desperate〔'dɛspərɪt〕*adj.* 絕望的

Poverty is an issue in parts of the world.	世界上有些地區有貧窮的問題。
Many people don't have anything to eat.	許多人沒有東西吃。
Many can't even find a place to sleep.	許多人甚至找不到地方睡覺。
Children long to go to school.	孩子們渴望去上學。
It is a farfetched dream to them.	對他們來說，那是無法實現的夢想。
It is a luxury they can't afford.	那是他們負擔不起的奢侈品。
Without education they can't improve.	不受教育，他們就無法進步。
They aren't able to care for themselves.	他們無法照顧自己。
They become a burden to the government.	他們變成政府的負擔。

** ────────────────────

issue〔ˈɪʃju〕 *n.* 問題　　***long to + V.*** 渴望～
farfetched〔ˈfɑrˈfɛtʃt〕 *adj.* 無法實現的
luxury〔ˈlʌkʃərɪ〕 *n.* 奢侈品　　afford〔əˈfɔrd〕 *v.* 負擔得起
improve〔ɪmˈpruv〕 *v.* 進步　　***be able to*** 能夠
care for 照顧　　burden〔ˈbɜdn̩〕 *n.* 負擔
government〔ˈgʌvənmənt〕 *n.* 政府

*I feel very fortunate compared
    to them.*

跟他們比，我覺得自己很
幸運。

I never worry about food or money.

我從不擔心食物或金錢。

I am provided with a good education.

我受到良好的教育。

I sympathize with the kids in India.

我很同情印度的小孩。

I want to pitch in to help them
    someday.

將來有一天，我要參加幫助
他們的行動。

I want to offer them some relief.

我想要提供他們一些救濟品。

Our country may not be the best.

我們的國家也許不是最棒的。

But most of us live quite
    comfortably.

但是我們大多數的人都過得
很舒服。

We are given the chance to pursue
    our dreams!

我們有追求夢想的機會！

** ————————————————

fortunate〔'fɔrtʃənɪt〕*adj.* 幸運的

compare〔kəm'pɛr〕*v.* 比較

compared to 和～相比（= *compared with*）

provide〔prə'vaɪd〕*v.* 提供；供應

sympathize〔'sɪmpə,θaɪz〕*v.* 同情　　**pitch in** 參加

someday〔'sʌm,de〕*adv.* 將來有一天

offer〔'ɔfɚ〕*v.* 提供　　relief〔rɪ'lif〕*n.* 救濟品

comfortably〔'kʌmfɚtəblɪ〕*adv.* 舒服地　　pursue〔pɚ'su〕*v.* 追求

英語即席演講 ❽

準備時間：2分鐘

演講時間：2分鐘

【資料來源：未來趨勢考題】

Speech 8

Here we see robots doing chores.

One day everyone will have robots.

One day they will alter our way of living.

A robot could complete many tasks.

It could clean for me when I am busy.

It could cook for me when I am hungry.

It could play with me when I am bored.

It could be my friend when I am sad.

It could give me advice when I am
    confused.

---

robot ('robət)   chores (tʃorz)

one day   alter ('ɔltə)

complete (kəm'plit)   task (tæsk)

bored (bord)   sad (sæd)

advice (əd'vaɪs)   confused (kən'fjuzd)

Robots could be custom-made.

Some may like tall and thin robots.

Some may prefer short and chubby ones.

They could also be fashionable.

I would buy my robot some accessories.

I would dress it in beautiful clothes.

They could be made for different
  purposes.

We could program them to sing with us.

We could program them to guard the
  doors.

custom-made〔'kʌstəm'med〕

thin〔θɪn〕   prefer〔prɪ'fɝ〕

chubby〔'tʃʌbɪ〕   fashionable〔'fæʃənəbl̩〕

accessories〔æk'sɛsərɪz〕   dress〔drɛs〕

purpose〔'pɝpəs〕   program〔'progræm〕

guard〔gɑrd〕

***Even so, robots can't take our place*.**

They can't feel emotions.

They can't contemplate things like
    we do.

Robots are still just machines.

They can't replace the human mind.

They can only take orders from us.

Technology may bring us advantages.

We should enjoy its convenience.

But we should not rely on it completely.

---

even so

emotion (ɪ'moʃən)

machine (mə'ʃin)

mind (maɪnd)

technology (tɛk'nɑlədʒɪ)

advantage (əd'væntɪdʒ)

rely (rɪ'laɪ)

completely (kəm'plitlɪ)

take *one's* ***place***

contemplate ('kɑntəm,plet)

replace (rɪ'ples)

order ('ɔrdɚ)

convenience (kən'vinjəns)

rely on

■ Speech 8

● 演講解說

Here we see robots doing chores.	我們看到機器人在做家事。
One day everyone will have robots.	有一天每個人都會有機器人。
One day they will alter our way of living.	有一天它們會改變我們的生活方式。
A robot could complete many tasks.	機器人可以完成許多任務。
It could clean for me when I am busy.	當我很忙時，它可以幫我打掃。
It could cook for me when I am hungry.	當我很餓時，它可以煮飯給我吃。
It could play with me when I am bored.	當我無聊時，它可以跟我玩。
It could be my friend when I am sad.	當我傷心時，它可以當我的朋友。
It could give me advice when I am confused.	當我困惑時，它可以給我建議。

** ─────────────────────

robot〔ˈrobət〕*n.* 機器人　　chores〔tʃorz〕*n. pl.* 雜事；家事
one day （將來或過去）有一天　　alter〔ˈɔltɚ〕*v.* 改變
complete〔kəmˈplit〕*v.* 完成　　task〔tæsk〕*n.* 任務；工作
bored〔bord〕*adj.* 無聊的　　sad〔sæd〕*adj.* 悲傷的
advice〔ədˈvaɪs〕*n.* 建議　　confused〔kənˈfjuzd〕*adj.* 困惑的

Robots could be custom-made.	我們可以訂做機器人。
Some may like tall and thin robots.	有些人可能喜歡高瘦型的機器人。
Some may prefer short and chubby ones.	有些人可能比較喜歡矮胖型的。
They could also be fashionable.	機器人也可以很時髦。
I would buy my robot some accessories.	我會買一些配件給我的機器人。
I would dress it in beautiful clothes.	我會爲它穿上美麗的衣服。
They could be made for different purposes.	它們可以依照不同的用途來製造。
We could program them to sing with us.	我們可以設定它們跟我們唱歌。
We could program them to guard the doors.	我們可以設定它們去守門。

** ————————————————

custom-made〔ˈkʌstəmˈmed〕*adj.* 訂做的

thin〔θɪn〕*adj.* 瘦的   prefer〔prɪˈfɝ〕*v.* 比較喜歡

chubby〔ˈtʃʌbɪ〕*adj.* 圓胖的

fashionable〔ˈfæʃənəbḷ〕*adj.* 時髦的

accessories〔ækˈsɛsərɪz〕*n. pl.* 配件

dress〔drɛs〕*v.* 給…穿衣服   purpose〔ˈpɝpəs〕*n.* 目的；用途

program〔ˈprogræm〕*v.* 設定程式   guard〔gɑrd〕*v.* 看守

Even so, *robots can't take our place*.

They can't feel emotions.

They can't contemplate things like we do.

Robots are still just machines.

They can't replace the human mind.

They can only take orders from us.

Technology may bring us advantages.

We should enjoy its convenience.

But we should not rely on it completely.

即使如此,機器人還是無法取代我們。

它們沒有情緒。

它們不能像我們一樣思考事情。

機器人仍然只是機器。

它們不能取代人腦。

它們只能接受我們的命令。

科技可能會帶給我們很多好處。

我們應該享受科技的便利。

但我們不應該完全依賴科技。

** ─────────────────

even so 即使如此　　***take one's place*** 取代某人

emotion〔ɪ'moʃən〕*n.* 情緒

contemplate〔'kɑntəm,plet〕*v.* 沉思;思考

machine〔mə'ʃin〕*n.* 機器　　replace〔rɪ'ples〕*v.* 取代

mind〔maɪnd〕*n.* 頭腦;想法　　order〔'ɔrdɚ〕*n.* 命令

technology〔tɛk'nɑlədʒɪ〕*n.* 科技

advantage〔əd'væntɪdʒ〕*n.* 優點;好處

convenience〔kən'vinjəns〕*n.* 便利　　rely〔rɪ'laɪ〕*v.* 依賴

rely on 依賴　　completely〔kəm'plitlɪ〕*adv.* 完全地

英語即席演講 ❾

準備時間：2分鐘

演講時間：2分鐘

【資料來源：社會時事考題】

Speech 9

Here is a man with a chubby dog.
He is being arrested.
He is being charged with mistreating his pet.

The dog is too fat.
It has been fed too much.
It is not healthy at all.

The man didn't realize he was doing
　something wrong.
He only wanted it to enjoy the food.
He did not wish to harm it.

chubby〔ˈtʃʌbɪ〕	arrest〔əˈrɛst〕
charge〔tʃɑrdʒ〕	*be charged with*
mistreat〔mɪsˈtrit〕	pet〔pɛt〕
feed〔fid〕	*not…at all*
healthy〔ˈhɛlθɪ〕	realize〔ˈriəˌlaɪz〕
wish〔wɪʃ〕	harm〔hɑrm〕

***Here are some facts we should know*.**

Many believe dogs are happy when fed.

But too much food may make them sick.

Dogs get excited at the sight of food.

***It*'s** because they don't know any better.

***It*'s** up to us to give them a healthy diet.

When overweight, they need to lose
weight.

When sick, they need to see a vet.

Keeping a dog is a big responsibility.

---

fact (fækt)	excited (ɪk'saɪtɪd)
sight (saɪt)	***at the sight of***
know better	***be up to*** sb.
diet ('daɪət)	overweight ('ovɚ'wet)
weight (wet)	***lose weight***
vet (vɛt)	keep (kip)
responsibility (rɪ͵spɑnsə'bɪlətɪ)	

People say a dog is a man's best friend.

They are our faithful companions.

They protect us in times of need.

We should love and cherish them.

We should help them stay fit.

We should not indulge them with food.

Dogs need to exercise as much as

  we do.

Take your dog for a walk daily.

Be a responsible owner!

man〔mæn〕	faithful〔ˈfeθfəl〕
companion〔kəmˈpænjən〕	protect〔prəˈtɛkt〕
in times of need	cherish〔ˈtʃɛrɪʃ〕
stay〔ste〕	fit〔fɪt〕
indulge〔ɪnˈdʌldʒ〕	
take ~ for a walk	daily〔ˈdelɪ〕
responsible〔rɪˈspɑnsəbḷ〕	owner〔ˈonɚ〕

■ Speech 9

● 演講解說

Here is a man with a chubby dog.	這裡有個男人和一隻胖狗。
He is being arrested.	那男人被逮捕了。
He is being charged with mistreating his pet.	他被控虐待寵物。
The dog is too fat.	這隻狗太胖了。
It has been fed too much.	牠被餵了太多東西。
It is not healthy at all.	牠一點都不健康。
The man didn't realize he was doing something wrong.	那個男人不知道自己做錯事了。
He only wanted it to enjoy the food.	他只是想讓那隻狗吃得開心。
He did not wish to harm it.	他並不想傷害牠。

＊＊ ─────────────────────

chubby〔ˈtʃʌbɪ〕*adj.* 圓胖的   arrest〔əˈrɛst〕*v.* 逮捕
charge〔tʃɑrdʒ〕*v.* 控告   *be charged with* 被指控
mistreat〔mɪsˈtrit〕*v.* 虐待   pet〔pɛt〕*n.* 寵物
feed〔fid〕*v.* 餵【三態變化為：feed-fed〔fɛd〕-fed】
not…at all 一點也不…   healthy〔ˈhɛlθɪ〕*adj.* 健康的
realize〔ˈrɪəˌlaɪz〕*v.* 了解   wish〔wɪʃ〕*v.* 希望；想
harm〔hɑrm〕*v.* 傷害

Here are some facts we should know.	有些事實我們應該要知道。
Many believe dogs are happy when fed.	許多人認為狗被餵食的時候很開心。
But too much food may make them sick.	但是太多食物會讓牠們生病。
Dogs get excited at the sight of food.	狗一看到食物就會很興奮。
It's because they don't know any better.	那是因為牠們懂的不夠多。
It's up to us to give them a healthy diet.	牠們能否擁有健康的飲食，取決於我們。
When overweight, they need to lose weight.	超重時，牠們需要減重。
When sick, they need to see a vet.	生病時，牠們需要看獸醫。
Keeping a dog is a big responsibility.	養狗是很大的責任。

** —————————————————

fact〔fækt〕n. 事實　　excited〔ɪkˈsaɪtɪd〕adj. 興奮的

sight〔saɪt〕n. 看見　　***at the sight of*** 一看到

know better 有頭腦；明事理（而不至於犯錯）

be up to sb. 取決於某人　　diet〔ˈdaɪət〕n. 飲食

overweight〔ˈovɚˈwet〕adj. 超重的　　weight〔wet〕n. 體重

lose weight 減重　　vet〔vɛt〕n. 獸醫（= *veterinarian*）

keep〔kip〕v. 飼養　　responsibility〔rɪˌspɑnsəˈbɪlətɪ〕n. 責任

People say a dog is a man's best friend.	人們說狗是人類最好的朋友。
They are our faithful companions.	牠們是我們忠實的同伴。
They protect us in times of need.	牠們會在緊急時刻保護我們。
We should love and cherish them.	我們應該愛護並珍惜牠們。
We should help them stay fit.	我們應該幫助牠們保持健康。
We should not indulge them with food.	我們不應該縱容牠們大吃大喝。
Dogs need to exercise as much as we do.	狗需要的運動量跟我們一樣多。
Take your dog for a walk daily.	要每天帶你的狗去散步。
Be a responsible owner!	要當個負責任的主人！

**　**──────────────────

man〔mæn〕*n.* 人　　faithful〔'feθfəl〕*adj.* 忠實的

companion〔kəm'pænjən〕*n.* 同伴

protect〔prə'tɛkt〕*v.* 保護

in times of need 在緊急時　　cherish〔'tʃɛrɪʃ〕*v.* 珍惜

stay〔ste〕*v.* 保持　　fit〔fɪt〕*adj.* 健康的

indulge〔ɪn'dʌldʒ〕*v.* 縱容；放任　　***take~for a walk*** 帶~去散步

daily〔'delɪ〕*adv.* 每天　　responsible〔rɪ'spɑnsəbḷ〕*adj.* 負責任的

owner〔'onɚ〕*n.* 所有人；物主

英語即席演講 ❿

準備時間：2 分鐘

演講時間：2 分鐘

【資料來源：和平高中高一即席演講比賽】

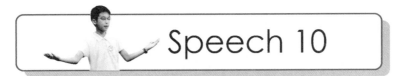

Speech 10

There is a big train station.
A little boy is lost.
He has been separated from his parents.

A police officer has found the little boy.
He is very concerned.
He wishes to help him.

The boy must be very frightened.
I know exactly how he feels.
I had a similar but different experience.

train station	lost (lɔst)
separate ('sɛpəˌret)	parents ('pɛrənts)
police officer	concerned (kən'sɝnd)
wish (wɪʃ)	frightened ('fraɪtn̩d)
exactly (ɪg'zæktlɪ)	similar ('sɪmələ˞)
different ('dɪfrənt)	experience (ɪk'spɪrɪəns)

This reminds me of when I was little.

I wandered off by myself in a busy market.

I did not panic and asked for help.

I stayed quite calm.

I did not make a scene.

I gave the officer my name and telephone number.

I was taught how to behave in a crisis.

My mom made sure I knew how to react.

I'm glad she educated me well.

remind〔rɪˋmaɪnd〕	wander〔ˋwɑndɚ〕
wander off	***by*** oneself
busy〔ˋbɪzɪ〕	market〔ˋmɑrkɪt〕
panic〔ˋpænɪk〕	***ask for***
stay〔ste〕	quite〔kwaɪt〕
calm〔kɑm〕	scene〔sin〕
make a scene	officer〔ˋɔfəsɚ〕
behave〔bɪˋhev〕	crisis〔ˋkraɪsɪs〕
make sure	react〔rɪˋækt〕
glad〔glæd〕	educate〔ˋɛdʒəˌket〕

It's important to watch over your kids.

Hold their hands tightly.

Don't let them out of your sight.

Kidnappings are reported every day.

Some kids are found.

Some unfortunately become victims of

    crimes.

Prevention is better than cure.

Don't leave room for regret.

Keep an eye on your child at all times!

important (ɪm'pɔrtn̩t)

watch over   kid (kɪd)

hold (hold)   tightly ('taɪtlɪ)

out of   sight (saɪt)

kidnapping ('kɪdnæpɪŋ)   report (rɪ'port)

unfortunately (ʌn'fɔrtʃənɪtlɪ)

victim ('vɪktɪm)   crime (kraɪm)

prevention (prɪ'vɛnʃən)   cure (kjʊr)

Prevention is better than cure.   leave (liv)

room (rum)   regret (rɪ'grɛt)

keep an eye on   ***at all times***

■ Speech 10

● 演講解說

There is a big train station. | 有一個很大的車站。
A little boy is lost. | 有個小男孩迷路了。
He has been separated from his parents. | 他和他的父母走散了。

A police officer has found the little boy. | 有位警察發現這個小男孩。
He is very concerned. | 他很擔心。
He wishes to help him. | 他想幫助他。

The boy must be very frightened. | 這個男孩一定很害怕。
I know exactly how he feels. | 我完全知道他的感覺。
I had a similar but different experience. | 我有過類似但不同的經驗。

**

train station 火車站　　lost〔lɔst〕*adj.* 迷路的
separate〔ˈsɛpəˌret〕*v.* 使分開　　parents〔ˈpɛrənts〕*n. pl.* 父母
police officer 警察　　concerned〔kənˈsɝnd〕*adj.* 擔心的
wish〔wɪʃ〕*v.* 希望；想　　frightened〔ˈfraɪtn̩d〕*adj.* 害怕的
exactly〔ɪgˈzæktlɪ〕*adv.* 確切地；完全地
similar〔ˈsɪmələ〕*adj.* 類似的　　different〔ˈdɪfrənt〕*adj.* 不同的
experience〔ɪkˈspɪrɪəns〕*n.* 經驗

This reminds me of when I was little.	這使我想起我小時候。
I wandered off by myself in a busy market.	我獨自在熱鬧的市場中走失。
I did not panic and asked for help.	我沒有驚慌和求助。
I stayed quite calm.	我保持得相當冷靜。
I did not make a scene.	我沒有大吵大鬧。
I gave the officer my name and telephone number.	我告訴警察我的名字和電話號碼。
I was taught how to behave in a crisis.	我有被教過遇到危機要怎麼做。
My mom made sure I knew how to react.	我媽媽確定我知道要如何反應。
I'm glad she educated me well.	我很高興她把我教育得很好。

＊＊ ─────────────

remind〔rɪˋmaɪnd〕*v.* 使想起　　wander〔ˋwɑndɚ〕*v.* 徘徊；迷路

wander off 與同伴走散；走失　　***by oneself*** 獨自

busy〔ˋbɪzɪ〕*adj.* 熱鬧的　　market〔ˋmɑrkɪt〕*n.* 市場

panic〔ˋpænɪk〕*v.* 驚慌　　***ask for*** 要求　　stay〔ste〕*v.* 保持

quite〔kwaɪt〕*adv.* 相當　　calm〔kɑm〕*adj.* 冷靜的

scene〔sin〕*n.* 場景；大吵大鬧　　***make a scene*** 大吵大鬧

officer〔ˋɔfəsɚ〕*n.* 警察　　behave〔bɪˋhev〕*v.* 行為舉止；表現

crisis〔ˋkraɪsɪs〕*n.* 危機　　***make sure*** 確定

react〔rɪˋækt〕*v.* 反應　　glad〔glæd〕*adj.* 高興的

educate〔ˋɛdʒə͵ket〕*v.* 教育

It's important to watch over your kids.	看護你的小孩很重要。
Hold their hands tightly.	要握緊他們的手。
Don't let them out of your sight.	不要讓他們離開你的視線。
Kidnappings are reported every day.	每天都有綁架的報導。
Some kids are found.	有些小孩被找到。
Some unfortunately become victims of crimes.	有些不幸成為犯罪的受害者。
Prevention is better than cure.	預防勝於治療。
Don't leave room for regret.	不要留下後悔的餘地。
Keep an eye on your child at all times!	要隨時留意你的小孩！

** ————————————————————

important〔ɪm'pɔrtṇt〕*adj.* 重要的　　***watch over*** 看護

kid〔kɪd〕*n.* 小孩　　hold〔hold〕*v.* 握住

tightly〔'taɪtlɪ〕*adv.* 緊緊地　　***out of*** 離開　　sight〔saɪt〕*n.* 視野

kidnapping〔'kɪdnæpɪŋ〕*n.* 綁架　　report〔rɪ'port〕*v.* 報導

unfortunately〔ʌn'fɔrtʃənɪtlɪ〕*adv.* 不幸地

victim〔'vɪktɪm〕*n.* 受害者　　crime〔kraɪm〕*n.* 犯罪

prevention〔prɪ'vɛnʃən〕*n.* 預防　　cure〔kjur〕*n.* 治療

Prevention is better than cure.　【諺】預防勝於治療。

leave〔liv〕*v.* 留下　　room〔rum〕*n.* 餘地；機會

regret〔rɪ'grɛt〕*n.* 後悔　　***keep an eye on*** 留意

at all times 隨時

英語即席演講 ⑪

準備時間：2分鐘

演講時間：2分鐘

【資料來源：建國高中高一即席演講比賽】

Speech 11

There's a man walking in the first picture.

He comes across a beggar on the street.

The beggar is asking for some money.

The beggar's face is covered in dirt.

His clothes are tattered and torn.

He's got a collection bowl in front of him.

The man is deciding what to do.

Should he help the beggar?

Or should he ignore him and walk away?

come across	beggar〔ˈbɛgɚ〕
ask for	cover〔ˈkʌvɚ〕
dirt〔dɝt〕	tattered〔ˈtætɚd〕
tear〔tɛr〕	***have got***
collection〔kəˈlɛkʃən〕	bowl〔bol〕
decide〔dɪˈsaɪd〕	ignore〔ɪgˈnor〕
walk away	

In the second picture, **the man decides**.

He reaches into his pocket and finds
  a dollar.

He walks over and gives it to the beggar.

The beggar is ecstatic.

"Thank you, kind sir!" the beggar shouts.

"You've really made my day!"

The kind man feels happy.

The kind man feels like he's really
  helped.

The kind man feels warmth in his heart.

---

reach (ritʃ)

walk over

kind (kaɪnd)

shout (ʃaʊt)

feel like

in one's heart

pocket ('pɑkɪt)

ecstatic (ɛk'stætɪk)

sir (sɜ˞)

make one's day

warmth (wɔrmθ)

But in the third picture, the man is

stunned.

The beggar gets up off the street.

Then he walks around the corner.

On the curb, there's a new BMW waiting.

The beggar gets inside the fancy car.

And then the beggar drives off!

The kind man doesn't know what to say.

The beggar was actually a rich man!

You really can't judge a book by

its cover!

stun〔stʌn〕	*get up*
off〔ɔf〕	around〔əˋraʊnd〕
corner〔ˋkɔrnɚ〕	curb〔kɝb〕
fancy〔ˋfænsɪ〕	*drive off*
actually〔ˋæktʃʊəlɪ〕	rich〔rɪtʃ〕
judge〔dʒʌdʒ〕	cover〔ˋkʌvɚ〕

You can't judge a book by its cover.

■ Speech 11

● 演講解說

There's a man walking in the first picture.	在第一張圖片中，有一位男士正在走路。
He comes across a beggar on the street.	他在街上遇到一個乞丐。
The beggar is asking for some money.	那個乞丐正在向他要錢。
The beggar's face is covered in dirt.	乞丐的臉上都是泥土。
His clothes are tattered and torn.	他的衣服都破破爛爛的。
He's got a collection bowl in front of him.	他前面有一個用來收錢的碗。
The man is deciding what to do.	這位男士正在決定該怎麼做。
Should he help the beggar?	他應該幫助那個乞丐嗎？
Or should he ignore him and walk away?	還是他應該不理會他，然後走開？

** ──────────────

come across 偶然遇到   beggar〔ˈbɛgɚ〕 *n.* 乞丐

ask for 要；要求   cover〔ˈkʌvɚ〕 *v.* 覆蓋   dirt〔dɝt〕 *n.* 泥土；污垢

tattered〔ˈtætɚd〕 *adj.* 破爛的   tear〔tɛr〕 *v.* 撕裂；扯破

have got 有   collection〔kəˈlɛkʃən〕 *n.* 收集

bowl〔bol〕 *n.* 碗   decide〔dɪˈsaɪd〕 *v.* 決定

ignore〔ɪgˈnor〕 *v.* 忽視；不理   *walk away* 走開

In the second picture, *the man decides*.

He reaches into his pocket and finds a dollar.

He walks over and gives it to the beggar.

在第二張圖片中，這位男士做出了決定。

他把手伸到口袋裡，找出一塊錢。

他走過去把錢給那個乞丐。

The beggar is ecstatic.

"Thank you, kind sir!" the beggar shouts.

"You've really made my day!"

那個乞丐欣喜若狂。

「謝謝你，好心的先生！」乞丐大喊。

「你真的讓我非常高興！」

The kind man feels happy.

The kind man feels like he's really helped.

The kind man feels warmth in his heart.

這位好心的先生覺得很高興。

這位好心的先生覺得乞丐真的有得到幫助。

這位好心的先生心裡覺得很溫暖。

** ————————————————

reach〔ritʃ〕*v.* 伸手　　pocket〔'pɑkɪt〕*n.* 口袋

walk over 走過去　　ecstatic〔ɛk'stætɪk〕*adj.* 欣喜若狂的

kind〔kaɪnd〕*adj.* 親切的；好心的　　sir〔sɝ〕*n.* 先生

shout〔ʃaʊt〕*v.* 喊叫　　*make one's day* 使某人非常高興

feel like 覺得好像　　warmth〔wɔrmθ〕*n.* 溫暖

in one's heart 在內心深處

But in the third picture, *the man is stunned*.

The beggar gets up off the street.

Then he walks around the corner.

On the curb, there's a new BMW waiting.

The beggar gets inside the fancy car.

And then the beggar drives off!

The kind man doesn't know what to say.

The beggar was actually a rich man!

You really can't judge a book by its cover!

但是在第三張圖片中，這位男士很吃驚。

乞丐起身離開了街道。

然後他繞過街角。

路邊有一台新的 BMW 在等著。

那個乞丐坐上那台高級汽車。

然後就開車離開！

這位好心的先生不知道該說些什麼。

那個乞丐竟然是個有錢人！

眞的是人不可貌相！

** ────────────

stun〔stʌn〕*v.* 使吃驚　　***get up*** 起身

off〔ɔf〕*prep.* 離開　　around〔əˈraʊnd〕*prep.* 繞過

corner〔ˈkɔrnɚ〕*n.* 轉角　　curb〔kɝb〕*n.*（人行道的）路緣；邊石

fancy〔ˈfænsɪ〕*adj.* 昂貴的；高級的　　***drive off*** 開車離開

actually〔ˈæktʃʊəlɪ〕*adv.* 事實上；竟然　　rich〔rɪtʃ〕*adj.* 有錢的

judge〔dʒʌdʒ〕*v.* 判斷　　cover〔ˈkʌvɚ〕*n.* 封面

You can't judge a book by its cover.【諺】不能憑封面判斷一本書；不可以貌取人。

英語即席演講 ⑫

準備時間：2分鐘

演講時間：2分鐘

【資料來源：建國高中高一即席演講比賽】

Speech 12

There's a girl in the first picture.

Her name is Jenny.

She's busy packing a picnic lunch.

Jenny is thinking about a picnic with Ted.

Ted is Jenny's boyfriend.

She's looking forward to a meal with Ted.

Jenny has prepared the picnic basket.

Jenny has made chicken and rice for
    lunch.

Jenny is hoping it will be a romantic meal.

be busy + V-ing   pack ﹝ pæk ﹞
picnic (ˈpɪknɪk)   *picnic lunch*
look forward to   meal ﹝ mil ﹞
prepare ﹝ prɪˈpɛr ﹞   basket (ˈbæskɪt)
chicken (ˈtʃɪkən)   rice ﹝ raɪs ﹞
romantic ﹝ roˈmæntɪk ﹞

Ted and Jenny are in the second picture.

They are both at the park.

They are sitting on a checkered

    blanket.

It is a beautiful day at the park.

It is autumn and leaves are falling.

The grass is green and lush.

Jenny reaches into the picnic basket.

She pulls out the lunch she prepared.

Ted can't wait to sink his teeth into it.

---

checkered ('tʃɛkəd)   blanket ('blæŋkɪt)

autumn ('ɔtəm)   leaves (livz)

fall (fɔl)   grass (græs)

lush (lʌʃ)   reach (ritʃ)

pull out

sink one's teeth into

But, *there's trouble in the third picture*.

Ted opens the lunch that Jenny made.

To their surprise, a big worm drops
　　inside!

It must have come from the tree.

It starts to eat their lunch.

Oh no, their lunch is ruined!

Ted is a little shocked.

Jenny is a little disappointed.

I guess they'll have to try again
　　another day!

trouble ('trʌbl̩)　　　　　　surprise (sə'praɪz)

to one's *surprise*　　　　　worm (wɝm)

drop (drɑp)　　　　　　　inside ('ɪn'saɪd)

must (mʌst)　　　　　　　ruin ('ruɪn)

shocked (ʃɑkt)

disappointed (ˌdɪsə'pɔɪntɪd)　　guess (gɛs)

■Speech 12

● 演講解說

There's a girl in the first picture.	在第一張圖片中，有個女孩。
Her name is Jenny.	她的名字是珍妮。
She's busy packing a picnic lunch.	她正忙著裝盒飯。
Jenny is thinking about a picnic with Ted.	珍妮想和泰德一起野餐。
Ted is Jenny's boyfriend.	泰德是珍妮的男朋友。
She's looking forward to a meal with Ted.	她很期待和泰德一起用餐。
Jenny has prepared the picnic basket.	珍妮已經準備了野餐籃。
Jenny has made chicken and rice for lunch.	珍妮已經做了雞肉和飯當午餐。
Jenny is hoping it will be a romantic meal.	珍妮希望那將會是很浪漫的一餐。

** ─────────────────

be busy + V-ing 忙於～   pack〔pæk〕*v.* 打包；裝填

picnic〔'pɪknɪk〕*n.* 野餐   *picnic lunch* 盒飯   *look forward to* 期待

meal〔mil〕*n.* 一餐   prepare〔prɪ'pɛr〕*v.* 準備

basket〔'bæskɪt〕*n.* 籃子   chicken〔'tʃɪkən〕*n.* 雞肉

rice〔raɪs〕*n.* 米飯   romantic〔ro'mæntɪk〕*adj.* 浪漫的

Ted and Jenny are in the second
  picture.

They are both at the park.

They are sitting on a checkered
  blanket.

在第二張圖片中，是泰德和
珍妮。

他們兩個都在公園裡。

他們正坐在有格子圖案的毯
子上。

It is a beautiful day at the park.

It is autumn and leaves are falling.

The grass is green and lush.

在公園裡，天氣很好。

現在是秋天，落葉紛紛。

草地很翠綠。

Jenny reaches into the picnic basket.

She pulls out the lunch she prepared.

Ted can't wait to sink his teeth
  into it.

珍妮把手伸進野餐籃裡。

她拿出她準備的午餐。

泰德等不及要咬一口。

** ─────────────────────────────

checkered〔ˈtʃɛkəd〕*adj.* 有格子圖案的

blanket〔ˈblæŋkɪt〕*n.* 毯子　　autumn〔ˈɔtəm〕*n.* 秋天

leaves〔livz〕*n. pl.* 葉子　　fall〔fɔl〕*v.* 落下

grass〔græs〕*n.* 草；草地　　lush〔lʌʃ〕*adj.* 嫩綠的；茂盛的

reach〔ritʃ〕*v.* 伸手　　*pull out* 拉出

sink one's teeth into 咬一口

But, *there's trouble in the third picture*.

但是在第三張圖片中，有麻煩了。

Ted opens the lunch that Jenny made.

泰德打開珍妮做的午餐。

To their surprise, a big worm drops inside!

令他們驚訝的是，有一隻大蟲掉到裡面！

It must have come from the tree.

牠一定是來自樹上。

It starts to eat their lunch.

牠開始吃他們的午餐。

Oh no, their lunch is ruined!

噢，糟糕，他們的午餐毀了！

Ted is a little shocked.

泰德有點震驚。

Jenny is a little disappointed.

珍妮有點失望。

I guess they'll have to try again another day!

我猜他們得改天再試一次！

** ——————————

trouble〔'trʌbḷ〕 *n.* 麻煩　　surprise〔sə'praɪz〕 *n.* 驚訝

to one's surprise 令某人驚訝的是

worm〔wɜm〕 *n.* 蟲　　drop〔drɑp〕 *v.* 掉落

inside〔'ɪn'saɪd〕 *adv.* 往裡面　　must〔mʌst〕 *aux.* 一定

ruin〔'ruɪn〕 *v.* 毀滅；破壞；毀掉

shocked〔ʃɑkt〕 *adj.* 震驚的

disappointed〔ˌdɪsə'pɔɪntɪd〕 *adj.* 失望的

guess〔gɛs〕 *v.* 猜

英語即席演講 ⑬

準備時間：2 分鐘

演講時間：2 分鐘

【資料來源：建國高中高二即席演講比賽】

Speech 13

In this picture, *three people are in a boat.*

Two seem to be arguing.

One of them looks a bit seasick.

The water looks very rough.

We can see many waves.

We can see water being splashed about.

The boat itself is going very fast.

But it is not smooth sailing at all.

The seasick man is getting dizzier.

seem〔sim〕

a bit

rough〔rʌf〕

splash〔splæʃ〕

go〔go〕

sailing〔'selɪŋ〕

dizzy〔'dɪzɪ〕

argue〔'ɑrgju〕

seasick〔'si,sɪk〕

wave〔wev〕

about〔ə'baʊt〕

smooth〔smuð〕

not…at all

It is a very interesting picture.

Some may think it is a scene from a

   movie.

But I think it is trying to tell us something.

I think the boat represents a team.

I think the people are the team members.

The water is the obstacle the team is

   facing.

The team is all together.

They are headed towards a common goal.

However, two of them are arguing.

---

scene〔sin〕

represent〔ˌrɛprɪ'zɛnt〕

member〔'mɛmbɚ〕

face〔fes〕

head〔hɛd〕

common〔'kɑmən〕

try〔traɪ〕

team〔tim〕

obstacle〔'ɑbstəkl̩〕

together〔tə'gɛðɚ〕

towards〔tə'wɔrdz〕

goal〔gol〕

One wants to go left.

The other wants to go right.

As a result, everyone is getting seasick.

To succeed, a team has to work together.

They have to agree on how to do things.

Disagreeing all the time will not help.

We can learn a lot from the picture.

Teams have to go in the same direction.

Otherwise, everyone will just get sick
and abandon ship!

left〔lɛft〕   right〔raɪt〕

as a result   succeed〔sək'sid〕

work together   agree〔ə'gri〕

disagree〔͵dɪsə'gri〕 ***all the time***

help〔hɛlp〕   direction〔də'rɛkʃən〕

otherwise〔'ʌðə͵waɪz〕 sick〔sɪk〕

get sick   abandon〔ə'bændən〕

■ Speech 13

● 演講解說

In this picture, *three people are in a boat*.	在這張圖中，有三個人在一艘船上。
Two seem to be arguing.	兩個人似乎在爭吵。
One of them looks a bit seasick.	其中一個看起來有點暈船。
The water looks very rough.	海水看起來很洶湧。
We can see many waves.	我們可以看到許多海浪。
We can see water being splashed about.	我們可以看到水花四濺。
The boat itself is going very fast.	這艘船本身行駛得很快。
But it is not smooth sailing at all.	但是航行得一點也不平穩。
The seasick man is getting dizzier.	暈船的男士頭更暈了。

**

seem〔sim〕*v.* 似乎   argue〔'ɑrgju〕*v.* 爭論   *a bit* 有點

seasick〔'si,sɪk〕*adj.* 暈船的   rough〔rʌf〕*adj.* 洶湧的

wave〔wev〕*n.* 海浪   splash〔splæʃ〕*v.* 使飛濺

about〔ə'baut〕*adv.* 到處   go〔go〕*v.* 前進

smooth〔smuð〕*adj.* 平穩的   sailing〔'selɪŋ〕*n.* 航行

not…at all 一點也不…   dizzy〔'dɪzɪ〕*adj.* 頭暈的

It is a very interesting picture.

Some may think it is a scene from
a movie.

But I think it is trying to tell us
something.

I think the boat represents a team.

I think the people are the team
members.

The water is the obstacle the team
is facing.

The team is all together.

They are headed towards a common
goal.

However, two of them are arguing.

這是一張很有趣的圖。

有些人可能認爲它是電影裡
的一個場景。

但是我認爲它想要告訴我們
一些事情。

我認爲這艘船象徵一個團隊。

我認爲這些人是團隊的成員。

海水是團隊面臨的阻礙。

團隊要共同合作。

他們朝著共同的目標前進。

然而，其中有兩個人卻在爭論。

** ——————————————

scene〔sin〕*n.* 場景　　try〔traɪ〕*v.* 試著；想要

represent〔ˏrɛprɪ'zɛnt〕*v.* 代表；象徵

team〔tim〕*n.* 隊　　member〔'mɛmbɚ〕*n.* 成員

obstacle〔'ɑbstəkl̩〕*n.* 阻礙　　face〔fes〕*v.* 面臨

together〔tə'gɛðɚ〕*adv.* 一起；合作

head〔hɛd〕*v.* 使前進　　towards〔tə'wɔrdz〕*prep.* 朝向

common〔'kɑmən〕*adj.* 共同的　　goal〔gol〕*n.* 目標

One wants to go left.	一個人想要往左。
The other wants to go right.	另一個人想要往右。
As a result, everyone is getting seasick.	結果，每個人都暈船了。
To succeed, a team has to work together.	為了成功，團隊必須合作。
They have to agree on how to do things.	關於事情要怎麼做，他們必須意見一致。
Disagreeing all the time will not help.	經常意見不合是沒有用的。
We can learn a lot from the picture.	我們可以從這張圖片學到很多。
Teams have to go in the same direction.	團隊必須朝同樣的方向前進。
Otherwise, everyone will just get sick and abandon ship!	否則，每個人就會覺得想嘔吐，並棄船而去！

**　——————————————————

left〔lɛft〕*adv.* 向左　　right〔raɪt〕*adv.* 向右

as a result 因此；結果　　succeed〔sək'sid〕*v.* 成功

work together 合作　　agree〔ə'gri〕*v.* 同意；意見一致

disagree〔ˏdɪsə'gri〕*v.* 不同意；意見不合

all the time 經常　　help〔hɛlp〕*v.* 有用；有幫助

direction〔də'rɛkʃən〕*n.* 方向　　otherwise〔'ʌðɚˏwaɪz〕*adv.* 否則

sick〔sɪk〕*adj.* 想嘔吐的　　*get sick* 覺得想嘔吐的

abandon〔ə'bændən〕*v.* 拋棄；放棄

英語即席演講 ⑭

準備時間：2 分鐘

演講時間：2 分鐘

【資料來源：建國高中高二即席演講比賽】

Speech 14

This is a picture of a scale.
On one side, we see a picture of a couple.
They are obviously deeply in love.

On the other side, we see a pile of food.
We can see muffins and loaves of bread.
The scale is completely balanced.

I think that this image is weird.
But if we look closer, it tells us something.
It asks us which is more important,
    love or money?

scale (skel)

couple ('kʌpḷ)

deeply ('diplɪ)

pile (paɪl)

loaf (lof)

balanced ('bælənst)

weird (wɪrd)

side (saɪd)

obviously ('ɑbvɪəslɪ)

be deeply in love

muffin ('mʌfɪn)

completely (kəm'plitlɪ)

image ('ɪmɪdʒ)

close (klos)

Some think that money is more

   important.

Some think that love is the right choice.

Let me tell you what I think.

We all need money to live.

After all, we all need to eat!

But I don't think money is the answer.

I think finding true love is more

   precious.

There are many people on this earth.

Finding the right one is tough!

choice〔tʃɔɪs〕	*after all*
answer〔'ænsɚ〕	precious〔'prɛʃəs〕
earth〔ɝθ〕	tough〔tʌf〕

***Yes*, *we need money to survive*.**

We can't do much without it.

But love cannot be bought.

***Love has to be* found.**

***Love has to be* nurtured.**

Finding true love is truly a miracle.

We can earn money many different ways.

But true love comes only once in a

   lifetime.

Never forget how truly precious love is!

---

survive 〔 səˈvaɪv 〕 nurture 〔ˈnɝtʃɚ 〕

truly 〔ˈtrulɪ 〕 miracle 〔ˈmɪrəkl̩ 〕

earn 〔 ɝn 〕 way 〔 we 〕

come 〔 kʌm 〕 once 〔 wʌns 〕

lifetime 〔ˈlaɪfˌtaɪm 〕

■ Speech 14

● 演講解說

This is a picture of a scale.　　　　　　這是一張天平的圖片。
On one side, we see a picture of a　　　在一邊,我們可以看到一對情
　couple.　　　　　　　　　　　　　侶的圖。
They are obviously deeply in love.　　他們顯然在熱戀中。

On the other side, we see a pile of food.　另一邊,我們看到一堆食物。
We can see muffins and loaves of　　　　我們可以看到鬆餅和一條條的
　bread.　　　　　　　　　　　　　麵包。
The scale is completely balanced.　　　天平是完全平衡的。

I think that this image is weird.　　　　我認為這張圖很奇怪。
But if we look closer, it tells us　　　　但如果我們看仔細一點,它是
　something.　　　　　　　　　　　要告訴我們某件事情。
It asks us which is more important,　　它在問我們哪個比較重要,愛
　love or money?　　　　　　　　　情還是金錢?

**

scale〔skel〕*n.* 天平　　side〔saɪd〕*n.* 邊
couple〔'kʌpl̩〕*n.*(一對)夫妻;情侶　　obviously〔'ɑbvɪəslɪ〕*adv.* 顯然
deeply〔'diplɪ〕*adv.* 深深地　　***be deeply in love*** 熱戀中
pile〔paɪl〕*n.* 一堆　　muffin〔'mʌfɪn〕*n.* 鬆餅
loaf〔lof〕*n.* 一條(麵包)　　completely〔kəm'plitlɪ〕*adv.* 完全地
balanced〔'bælənst〕*adj.* 平衡的　　image〔'ɪmɪdʒ〕*n.* 圖像
weird〔wɪrd〕*adj.* 奇怪的　　close〔klos〕*adv.* 接近地

Some think that money is more important.

Some think that love is the right choice.

Let me tell you what I think.

We all need money to live.

After all, we all need to eat!

But I don't think money is the answer.

I think finding true love is more precious.

There are many people on this earth.

Finding the right one is tough!

有些人認為金錢比較重要。

有些人認為愛情才是正確的選擇。

讓我告訴你們我的想法。

我們都需要錢生活。

畢竟,我們都需要吃東西!

但我不認為金錢就是解決辦法。

我認為找到真愛更珍貴。

地球上有許多人。

要找到對的人很難!

**

choice〔tʃɔɪs〕*n.* 選擇   ***after all*** 畢竟
answer〔'ænsɚ〕*n.* 答案;解決辦法
precious〔'prɛʃəs〕*adj.* 珍貴的
earth〔ɝθ〕*n.* 地球   tough〔tʌf〕*adj.* 困難的

Yes, *we need money to survive*.　　　是的，我們需要錢才能生存。

We can't do much without it.　　　如果沒有錢，我們很多事都不能做。

But love cannot be bought.　　　但是愛情是買不到的。

Love has to be found.　　　愛情必須去尋找。

Love has to be nurtured.　　　愛情必須要培養。

Finding true love is truly a　　　能找到真愛真的是一個奇蹟。
　　miracle.

We can earn money many　　　我們可以用很多不同的方法賺錢。
　　different ways.

But true love comes only once　　　但是真愛一生只出現一次。
　　in a lifetime.

Never forget how truly precious　　　絕不要忘記愛情有多珍貴！
　　love is!

** ————————————————

survive〔sə'vaɪv〕*v.* 存活

nurture〔'nɝtʃɚ〕*v.* 養育；培養

truly〔'trulɪ〕*adv.* 真正地　　miracle〔'mɪrəkl̩〕*n.* 奇蹟

earn〔ɝn〕*v.* 賺　　way〔we〕*n.* 方法

come〔kʌm〕*v.* 出現　　once〔wʌns〕*adv.* 一次

lifetime〔'laɪf͵taɪm〕*n.* 一生

英語即席演講 ⑮

準備時間：2分鐘

演講時間：2分鐘

【資料來源：建國高中高二即席演講比賽】

Speech 15

The picture is of a funeral.
There is a priest on the left.
There is a coffin beside him.

The woman in the middle is very sad.
A single tear runs down her cheek.
She seems to have known the deceased
very well.

It is a very solemn ceremony.
Everyone there is mourning.
The priest is trying to comfort everyone.

funeral (ˈfjunərəl)
coffin (ˈkɔfɪn)
middle (ˈmɪdl̩)
tear (tɪr)
cheek (tʃik)
deceased (dɪˈsist)
solemn (ˈsɑləm)
mourn (morn)

priest (prist)
beside (bɪˈsaɪd)
single (ˈsɪŋgl̩)
run down
seem (sim)
the deceased
ceremony (ˈsɛrəˌmonɪ)
comfort (ˈkʌmfət)

When I look at this picture,

   I feel sad, too.

I feel sorry for the woman.

She looks very depressed.

It seems she has regrets.

Maybe she regrets what she said.

Or maybe she regrets what she

   didn't say.

But now, it's too late.

The person is gone.

And there's nothing anyone can do.

sorry ('sɔrɪ)   depressed (dɪ'prɛst)

regret (rɪ'grɛt)   gone (gɔn)

Death is a part of life.

Everyone has to go at some point.

All we can do is live the best life we can.

We should tell people how we feel.

We can't wait too long.

Or else we could end up regretful.

Don't be afraid to share your feelings.

No one knows what tomorrow will bring.

Live each day to the fullest!

some〔sʌm〕　　　　　　point〔pɔɪnt〕
All one can do is + V.
live the best life we can　　***or else***
end up　　　　　　regretful〔rɪ'grɛtfḷ〕
share〔ʃɛr〕　　　　　　feelings〔'filɪŋz〕
tomorrow〔tə'mɔro〕　　bring〔brɪŋ〕
what tomorrow will bring
to the full

■Speech 15

● 演講解說

The picture is of a funeral.	這是一張葬禮的圖片。
There is a priest on the left.	左邊有一位神父。
There is a coffin beside him.	他旁邊有一具棺材。
The woman in the middle is very sad.	中間那位女士很悲傷。
A single tear runs down her cheek.	有一滴眼淚流下她的臉頰。
She seems to have known the deceased very well.	她似乎和死者很熟。
It is a very solemn ceremony.	這是一個非常莊嚴的典禮。
Everyone there is mourning.	在那裡的每個人都在哀悼。
The priest is trying to comfort everyone.	神父試著要安慰大家。

** ────────────────────

funeral〔'fjunərəl〕*n.* 葬禮   priest〔prist〕*n.* 神父
coffin〔'kɔfɪn〕*n.* 棺材   beside〔bɪ'saɪd〕*prep.* 在…旁邊
middle〔'mɪdl̩〕*n.* 中間   single〔'sɪŋgl̩〕*adj.* 單一的
tear〔tɪr〕*n.* 眼淚   ***run down*** 流下   cheek〔tʃik〕*n.* 臉頰
seem〔sim〕*v.* 似乎   deceased〔dɪ'sist〕*adj.* 死亡的
the deceased 死者   solemn〔'sɑləm〕*adj.* 嚴肅的；莊嚴的
ceremony〔'sɛrə,monɪ〕*n.* 典禮
mourn〔morn〕*v.* 哀悼   comfort〔'kʌmfɚt〕*v.* 安慰

When I look at this picture, ***I feel***
sad, ***too***.

I feel sorry for the woman.

She looks very depressed.

It seems she has regrets.

Maybe she regrets what she said.

Or maybe she regrets what she
　didn't say.

But now, it's too late.

The person is gone.

And there's nothing anyone
　can do.

當我看到這張圖片時，我也感
到很悲傷。

我爲這位女士感到難過。

她看起來很沮喪。

她看起來很後悔。

她可能爲她所說的話感到後悔。

或可能爲她還沒說的話感到
後悔。

但是現在一切都太晚了。

這個人已經過世了。

任何人都無能爲力。

** ────────────────────

sorry〔'sɔrɪ〕*adj.* 感到難過的

depressed〔dɪ'prɛst〕*adj.* 沮喪的

regret〔rɪ'grɛt〕*n. v.* 後悔　　gone〔gɔn〕*adj.* 已死的

Death is a part of life.	死亡是生命的一部分。
Everyone has to go at some point.	每個人在某個時刻都一定會走。
All we can do is live the best life we can.	我們所能做的，就是盡可能好好過生活。
We should tell people how we feel.	我們應該告訴別人我們的感受。
We can't wait too long.	我們不可以等待太久。
Or else we could end up regretful.	否則我們最後會後悔。
Don't be afraid to share your feelings.	不要害怕分享你的感情。
No one knows what tomorrow will bring.	沒有人知道未來會發生什麼事。
Live each day to the fullest!	盡情地過每一天吧！

** ——————————————————

some〔sʌm〕*adj.* 某個   point〔pɔɪnt〕*n.*（特定的）時刻

***All one can do is* + *V*.** 某人所能做的就是…

live the best life we can 盡可能好好過生活（= *live as well as*
  we can）   ***or else*** 否則   ***end up*** 最後…

regretful〔rɪˈgrɛtfḷ〕*adj.* 後悔的

share〔ʃɛr〕*v.* 分享   feelings〔ˈfilɪŋz〕*n. pl.* 感情

tomorrow〔təˈmɔro〕*n.* 將來；未來   bring〔brɪŋ〕*v.* 使發生

what tomorrow will bring 未來會發生什麼事（= *what will*
  happen in the future）   ***to the full*** 充分地；盡情地

英語即席演講 ⓰

準備時間：5 分鐘

演講時間：2～3 分鐘

【資料來源：台北縣國民中小學英語競賽國小組】

Speech 16

Welcome, my dear friends.
It's wonderful to see you here.
Thank you for your attention.

Traveling is always interesting.
But traveling with our family is even
  better.
It can be a lot of fun.

Recently, my friend Jimmy went on a trip.
He went to Kaohsiung with his parents.
Here's what he told me.

wonderful ('wʌndɚfəl)   attention (ə'tɛnʃən)
traveling ('trævḷɪŋ)   interesting ('ɪntrɪstɪŋ)
travel ('trævḷ)   even ('ivən)
be a lot of fun   recently ('risṇtlɪ)
go on a trip

Jimmy and his parents got up very early.

Their train was leaving at 9:00.

Jimmy didn't want to be late.

He packed up his things.

He got in the car.

Before long, they were at the train
 station.

Jimmy was taking the high-speed rail.

He was really looking forward to
 the trip.

It was his very first time on a train.

get up	leave〔liv〕
pack up	*get in*
before long	train〔tren〕
train station	high-speed〔'haɪˌspid〕
rail〔rel〕	*high-speed rail*
look forward to	very〔'vɛrɪ〕

***At 9:00 sharp**, the train began to move*.

It started slowly at first.

After a few minutes, it reached top

  speed.

Jimmy looked out the window.

Buildings and trees were just

  whizzing by.

The new high-speed trains sure are quick!

Jimmy was very excited.

The high-speed train is a lot of fun.

In just a few hours, they would be there!

---

sharp (ʃɑrp)	move (muv)
start (stɑrt)	*at first*
reach (ritʃ)	top (tɑp)
speed (spid)	building ('bɪldɪŋ)
whiz (hwɪz)	sure (ʃur)
quick (kwɪk)	excited (ɪk'saɪtɪd)

By noon, Jimmy and his parents had arrived.

Kaohsiung was incredibly sunny.

It was a beautiful day.

They strolled along Love River.

They ate seafood in the Chijin District.

They even got to ride the harbor ferry.

But before long, it was time to go back.

Jimmy could hardly believe it.

Time certainly flies when we're having fun!

---

by noon

sunny ('sʌnɪ)

along (ə'lɔŋ)

district ('dɪstrɪkt)

ride (raɪd)

ferry ('fɛrɪ)

certainly ('sɝtṇlɪ)

have fun

incredibly (ɪn'krɛdəblɪ)

stroll (strol)

seafood ('si,fud)

get to

harbor ('hɑrbɚ)

hardly ('hɑrdlɪ)

fly (flaɪ)

By 6:00**, **they were back in Taipei City.

They got into their car and headed home.

It was an amazing time for Jimmy.

He went on a high-speed train ride.

He got to go to the very south of Taiwan.

He spent some quality time with his
 family.

Jimmy thanked his parents for a
 great day.

He had a fantastic experience.

He also learned a lot about Kaohsiung.

---

get into

amazing (ə'mezɪŋ)

spend (spɛnd)

quality ('kwɑlətɪ)

fantastic (fæn'tæstɪk)

experience (ɪk'spɪrɪəns)

head (hɛd)

south (saʊθ)

great (gret)

Jimmy's trip taught him a lot.

But who says we can't do the

same thing?

A short trip could be just what we need.

Traveling broadens our horizons.

We get to see new sights.

We get to try new things.

Make a plan to travel soon.

There are many places to visit.

A new adventure is right around the

corner!

---

broaden ('brɔdn̩)

horizons (hə'raɪzn̩z)　　　sight (saɪt)

plan (plæn)

adventure (əd'vɛntʃɚ)　　　right (raɪt)

corner ('kɔrnɚ)

around the corner

■ **Speech 16** ★

● 演講解説

Welcome, *my dear friends*.	歡迎，我親愛的朋友們。
It's wonderful to see you here.	能在這裡看到你們眞好。
Thank you for your attention.	謝謝你們專心聽我演講。
Traveling is always interesting.	旅遊總是很有趣。
But traveling with our family is even better.	但是和自己的家人一起旅行更棒。
It can be a lot of fun.	那可能會很有趣。
Recently, my friend Jimmy went on a trip.	最近，我的朋友吉米去旅行。
He went to Kaohsiung with his parents.	他和他的父母去高雄。
Here's what he told me.	以下是他告訴我的。

** ———————————————

wonderful〔'wʌndəfəl〕*adj.* 極好的；很棒的

attention〔ə'tɛnʃən〕*n.* 注意；專心

traveling〔'trævḷɪŋ〕*n.* 旅行

interesting〔'ɪntrɪstɪŋ〕*adj.* 有趣的   travel〔'trævḷ〕*v.* 旅行

even〔'ivən〕*adv.* 甚至；更加   ***be a lot of fun*** 很有趣

recently〔'risṇtlɪ〕*adv.* 最近   ***go on a trip*** 去旅行

***Jimmy and his parents got up very
    early*.** | 吉米和他的父母很早就起床。

Their train was leaving at 9:00. | 他們的列車在九點出發。

Jimmy didn't want to be late. | 吉米不想遲到。

He packed up his things. | 他把自己的東西打包好。

He got in the car. | 他坐上車。

Before long, they were at the train
    station. | 不久，他們就到了車站。

Jimmy was taking the high-speed rail. | 吉米搭高鐵。

He was really looking forward to the
    trip. | 他真的很期待這次的旅行。

It was his very first time on a train. | 這正是他第一次搭列車。

** ——————————————————

get up 起床　　leave〔liv〕*v.* 出發

pack up 打包　　*get in* 上（車）　　*before long* 不久

train〔tren〕*n.* 火車；列車　　*train station* 火車站

high-speed〔'haɪ,spid〕*adj.* 高速的

rail〔rel〕*n.* 鐵路　　*high-speed rail* 高鐵

look forward to 期待

very〔'vɛrɪ〕*adv.* 真正地；正是

***At 9:00 sharp**, **the train began to move**.*	九點整的時候，列車開始行進。
It started slowly at first.	它起先發動得很慢。
After a few minutes, it reached top speed.	幾分鐘後，它就達到最高的速度。
Jimmy looked out the window.	吉米往窗外看。
Buildings and trees were just whizzing by.	建築物和樹木從旁邊呼嘯而過。
The new high-speed trains sure are quick!	新的高鐵的確很快！
Jimmy was very excited.	吉米很興奮。
The high-speed train is a lot of fun.	高鐵很有趣。
In just a few hours, they would be there!	只要幾個小時，他們就會到那裡！

**   ————————————

sharp〔ʃɑrp〕*adv.* 整   move〔muv〕*v.* 移動

start〔stɑrt〕*v.* 發動   *at first* 起先

reach〔ritʃ〕*v.* 達到   top〔tɑp〕*adj.* 最高的

speed〔spid〕*n.* 速度   building〔'bɪldɪŋ〕*n.* 建築物

whiz〔hwɪz〕*v.* 颼颼地移動   sure〔ʃur〕*adv.* 的確

quick〔kwɪk〕*adj.* 快的   excited〔ɪk'saɪtɪd〕*adj.* 興奮的

***By noon**, **Jimmy and his parents** **had arrived**.*	到中午時，吉米和他的父母就抵達了。
Kaohsiung was incredibly sunny.	高雄非常晴朗。
It was a beautiful day.	天氣很好。
They strolled along Love River.	他們沿著愛河散步。
They ate seafood in the Chijin District.	他們在旗津吃海鮮。
They even got to ride the harbor ferry.	他們甚至搭了港口的渡輪。
But before long, it was time to go back.	但是不久，就是該回家的時候了。
Jimmy could hardly believe it.	吉米幾乎無法相信。
Time certainly flies when we're having fun!	當我們玩得愉快的時候，時間一定都過得很快！

** ——————————————

by noon 到了中午　　incredibly〔ɪnˈkrɛdəblɪ〕*adv.* 非常地
sunny〔ˈsʌnɪ〕*adj.* 晴朗的　　stroll〔strol〕*v.* 散步
along〔əˈlɔŋ〕*prep.* 沿著　　seafood〔ˈsiˌfud〕*n.* 海鮮
district〔ˈdɪstrɪkt〕*n.* 地區
get to 得以；能夠　　ride〔raɪd〕*v.* 搭乘
harbor〔ˈhɑrbɚ〕*n.* 港口　　ferry〔ˈfɛrɪ〕*n.* 渡輪
hardly〔ˈhɑrdlɪ〕*adv.* 幾乎不
certainly〔ˈsɝtn̩lɪ〕*adv.* 一定
fly〔flaɪ〕*v.*（時間）飛逝　　***have fun*** 玩得愉快

By 6:00**, **they were back in Taipei City.   到六點時,他們回到了台北。

They got into their car and headed   他們坐上車,並開回家。
  home.

It was an amazing time for   對吉米來說,這是一段非常開
  Jimmy.   心的時光。

He went on a high-speed train ride.   他搭乘了高鐵。

He got to go to the very south of   他能去到台灣最南部的地方。
  Taiwan.

He spent some quality time with   他和家人度過了很美好的時光。
  his family.

Jimmy thanked his parents for a   吉米為這很棒的一天感謝他的
  great day.   父母。

He had a fantastic experience.   他有一個很棒的經驗。

He also learned a lot about   他也知道許多關於高雄的事。
  Kaohsiung.

**

---

get into 上(車)   head〔hɛd〕*v.* (朝…的方向)前進

amazing〔ə'mezɪŋ〕*adj.* 驚人的;令人高興的

very〔'vɛrɪ〕*adj.* 最…的   south〔sauθ〕*n.* 南部

spend〔spɛnd〕*v.* 度過(時間)   quality〔'kwɑlətɪ〕*adj.* 極好的

great〔gret〕*adj.* 很棒的   fantastic〔fæn'tæstɪk〕*adj.* 很棒的

experience〔ɪk'spɪrɪəns〕*n.* 經驗

Jimmy's trip taught him a lot.

But who says we can't do the
same thing?

A short trip could be just what we
need.

吉米的旅行教了他很多。

但誰說我們不能做同樣的事情？

一趟短程的旅行可能正是我們
需要的。

Traveling broadens our horizons.

We get to see new sights.

We get to try new things.

旅行能拓展我們的眼界。

我們能看到新的景點。

我們能嘗試新的事物。

Make a plan to travel soon.

There are many places to visit.

*A new adventure is right around
the corner!*

馬上擬定旅行計畫。

有許多地方可以遊覽。

新的冒險馬上就要來臨了！

** ─────────────────────

broaden 〔'brɔdn̩〕 v. 拓展

horizons 〔 hə'raɪznz 〕 n. pl. 眼界；知識範圍

sight 〔 saɪt 〕 n. 景象　　 plan 〔 plæn 〕 n. 計畫

adventure 〔 əd'vɛntʃɚ 〕 n. 冒險

right 〔 raɪt 〕 adv. 正好；就

corner 〔'kɔrnɚ 〕 n. 角落

around the corner 即將來臨

英語即席演講 ⑰

準備時間：5 分鐘

演講時間：2～3 分鐘

【資料來源：台北縣國民中小學英語競賽國小組】

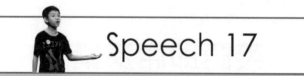

Speech 17

Dear friends and honored guests.
I would like to welcome all of you here.
I hope that you enjoy today's presentation.

Malls are quite amazing.
They've got so many things to see and buy.
They are always so crowded.

But what happens if we get lost?
It happened to my friend Bill once.
Let me tell you about it.

honored (ˈɑnəd)	guest (ɡɛst)
honored guest	***would like***
presentation (ˌprɛznˈteʃən)	mall (mɔl)
quite (kwaɪt)	amazing (əˈmezɪŋ)
have got	crowded (ˈkraʊdɪd)
get lost	once (wʌns)

Bill went to the mall with his mom.

He brought along his toy plane.

It was a gift from his uncle.

Bill loved that toy plane very much.

He almost always had it with him.

He dreamed about being a pilot

    one day.

Bill's mom went to look at some

    clothing.

But Bill just kept playing with his toy.

He was really into it.

along (əˈlɔŋ)　　　　　　toy (tɔɪ)

plane (plen)　　　　　　gift (gɪft)

uncle (ˈʌŋk!̩)　　　　　　dream (drim)

pilot (ˈpaɪlət)　　　　　　*one day*

clothing (ˈkloðɪŋ)　　　　keep (kip)

be into　　　　　　　　really (ˈriəlɪ)

Suddenly, Bill looked up.

He tried to find his mom.

But she was nowhere to be found.

He looked to the left, but she

    wasn't there.

He looked to the right, but nothing.

Bill started to panic.

He kept looking, but couldn't find her.

A terrible feeling started to come

    over him.

Bill realized that he was lost.

suddenly (ˈsʌdn̩lɪ)	*look up*
nowhere (ˈnoˌhwɛr)	*look to*
left (lɛft)	right (raɪt)
panic (ˈpænɪk)	terrible (ˈtɛrəbl̩)
feeling (ˈfilɪŋ)	*come over*
realize (ˈriəˌlaɪz)	

***Bill was really scared*.**

He didn't know what to do next.

He felt himself start to cry.

Then, a nice lady came over to him.

"Are you lost?" the lady asked.

"Yes," Bill sobbed.

"Don't worry," said the lady.

The lady took Bill to the information

   booth.

Then she made a public announcement.

---

scared (skɛrd)   next (nɛkst)

come over to   sob (sɑb)

booth (buθ)   ***information booth***

public ('pʌblɪk)

announcement (ə'naʊnsmənt)

public announcement

***A few minutes later*, *Bill's mom appeared*.**

"Bill!" shouted Bill's mom.

"Mom!" yelled Bill.

Bill's mom was relieved to find

   Bill again.

She had been looking all over for him.

Luckily, the nice lady was there to help.

Bill and his mom thanked the nice lady.

It was time for them to go home.

Bill vowed to pay more attention

   next time.

---

later〔ˈletɚ〕	appear〔əˈpɪr〕
shout〔ʃaʊt〕	yell〔jɛl〕
relieved〔rɪˈlivd〕	***all over***
luckily〔ˈlʌkɪlɪ〕	vow〔vaʊ〕
pay attention	***next time***

***In conclusion**, getting lost is not fun at all*.

It is a terrifying experience.

But there are a few things we can do.

If we get lost, we should stay calm.

We can look for an information desk.

We can ask a police officer for assistance.

***Try not to lose your head**.*

***Keep your wits about you**.*

Be smart and you will find your way!

---

conclusion (kən'kluʒən)	*in conclusion*
not···at all	fun (fʌn)
terrifying ('tɛrə,faɪɪŋ)	
experience (ɪk'spɪrɪəns)	stay (ste)
calm (kɑm)	*information desk*
police officer	assistance (ə'sɪstəns)
lose one's head	wit (wɪt)
keep one's wits about one	
smart (smɑrt)	way (we)

■ Speech 17

● 演講解說

Dear friends and honored guests.	親愛的朋友和貴賓。
I would like to welcome all of you here.	我想要歡迎大家來到這裡。
I hope that you enjoy today's presentation.	我希望你們會喜歡今天的演講。
Malls are quite amazing.	購物中心相當棒。
They've got so many things to see and buy.	它們有許多東西可以看和買。
They are always so crowded.	那裡總是很擁擠。
But what happens if we get lost?	但是如果我們迷路的話，會發生什麼事呢？
It happened to my friend Bill once.	它曾經在我的朋友比爾身上發生過一次。
Let me tell you about it.	讓我來告訴你們這件事。

** ─────────────

honored〔ˊɑnəd〕*adj.* 有名譽的　　guest〔gɛst〕*n.* 客人；來賓
honored guest 貴賓　　***would like*** 想要
presentation〔͵prɛznˊteʃən〕*n.* 演講　　mall〔mɔl〕*n.* 購物中心
quite〔kwaɪt〕*adv.* 相當　　amazing〔əˊmezɪŋ〕*adj.* 驚人的
have got 有　　crowded〔ˊkraʊdɪd〕*adj.* 擁擠的
get lost 迷路　　once〔wʌns〕*adv.* 一次

Bill went to the mall with his mom.	比爾和媽媽到購物中心去。
He brought along his toy plane.	他帶著他的玩具飛機一起去。
It was a gift from his uncle.	玩具飛機是叔叔給他的禮物。
Bill loved that toy plane very much.	比爾非常喜愛那個玩具飛機。
He almost always had it with him.	他幾乎總是帶在身邊。
He dreamed about being a pilot one day.	他夢想有一天能成為飛行員。
Bill's mom went to look at some clothing.	比爾的媽媽去看一些衣服。
But Bill just kept playing with his toy.	但比爾只是一直玩他的玩具。
He was really into it.	他真的很喜歡它。

** ─────────────────────────

along〔ə'lɔŋ〕*adv.* 一起

toy〔tɔɪ〕*adj.* 玩具的 *n.* 玩具   plane〔plen〕*n.* 飛機

gift〔gɪft〕*n.* 禮物   uncle〔'ʌŋkl̩〕*n.* 叔叔

dream〔drim〕*v.* 夢想   pilot〔'paɪlət〕*n.* 飛行員

one day （將來）有一天   clothing〔'kloðɪŋ〕*n.* 衣服

keep〔kip〕*v.* 持續；一直

be into 對…很有興趣；很喜歡   really〔'riəlɪ〕*adv.* 真正地

Suddenly, *Bill looked up*.　　　　　　突然間，比爾抬頭往上看。

He tried to find his mom.　　　　　　他試著找他的媽媽。

But she was nowhere to be found.　　　但是到處都找不到她。

He looked to the left, but she wasn't　　他往左看，但是她不在那裡。
　　there.

He looked to the right, but nothing.　　他往右看，但是什麼都沒有。

Bill started to panic.　　　　　　　比爾開始驚慌了。

He kept looking, but couldn't find her.　他一直找，但是無法找到她。

A terrible feeling started to come　　　他開始有一種很可怕的感覺。
　　over him.

Bill realized that he was lost.　　　　比爾知道他迷路了。

**

suddenly〔'sʌdn̩lɪ〕*adv.* 突然地　　***look up*** 抬頭看

nowhere〔'no͵hwɛr〕*adv.* 任何地方都不

look to 朝…看　　left〔lɛft〕*n.* 左邊

right〔raɪt〕*n.* 右邊　　panic〔'pænɪk〕*v.* 驚慌

terrible〔'tɛrəbl̩〕*adj.* 可怕的

feeling〔'filɪŋ〕*n.* 感覺

come over （感情等）侵襲；突然感到

realize〔'riə͵laɪz〕*v.* 了解；知道

Bill was really scared.	比爾真的很害怕。
He didn't know what to do next.	他不知道接下來該怎麼辦。
He felt himself start to cry.	他覺得自己開始哭了。
Then, a nice lady came over to him.	接著，一位好心的小姐向他走過來。
"Are you lost?" the lady asked.	「你迷路了嗎？」那位小姐問。
"Yes," Bill sobbed.	「是的，」比爾嗚咽著說。
"Don't worry," said the lady.	「不要擔心，」那位小姐說。
The lady took Bill to the information booth.	那位小姐帶比爾到服務台。
Then she made a public announcement.	然後她廣播。

** ─────────────────

scared〔skɛrd〕*adj.* 害怕的   next〔nɛkst〕*adv.* 接下來
come over to 朝…過來   sob〔sɑb〕*v.* 嗚咽著說
booth〔buθ〕*n.* 攤亭；崗亭
information booth 服務台；詢問處
public〔ˈpʌblɪk〕*adj.* 公開的
announcement〔əˈnaʊnsmənt〕*n.* 宣佈
public announcement 廣播

A few minutes later, *Bill's mom*
    appeared.
"Bill!" shouted Bill's mom.
"Mom!" yelled Bill.

Bill's mom was relieved to find Bill
    again.
She had been looking all over for him.
Luckily, the nice lady was there to
    help.

Bill and his mom thanked the nice
    lady.
It was time for them to go home.
Bill vowed to pay more attention next
    time.

幾分鐘之後，比爾的媽媽出
現了。
「比爾！」比爾的媽媽大喊。
「媽媽！」比爾大叫。

比爾的媽媽找回比爾，就放
心了。
她一直在四處找他。
幸好，這位好心的小姐在那
裡幫忙。

比爾和他的媽媽感謝這位好
心的小姐。
是他們該回家的時候了。
比爾發誓下次會更注意一點。

**

later〔'letɚ〕*adv.* ～之後　　appear〔ə'pɪr〕*v.* 出現
shout〔ʃaʊt〕*v.* 喊叫　　yell〔jɛl〕*v.* 大叫
relieved〔rɪ'livd〕*adj.* 放心的；鬆了一口氣的
all over 到處　　luckily〔'lʌkɪlɪ〕*adv.* 幸好
vow〔vaʊ〕*v.* 發誓　　*pay attention* 注意
next time 下次

In conclusion, **getting lost is not fun**
 at all. | 總之，迷路一點也不好玩。

It is a terrifying experience. | 那是個可怕的經驗。

But there are a few things we can do. | 但有幾件事是我們可以做的。

If we get lost, we should stay
 calm. | 如果我們迷路了，應該要保持冷靜。

We can look for an information desk. | 我們可以找服務台。

We can ask a police officer for
 assistance. | 我們可以請警察幫忙。

Try not to lose your head. | 試著不要慌張。

Keep your wits about you. | 要保持冷靜。

Be smart and you will find your way! | 如果你聰明一點，就會找到路！

** ───────────────────

conclusion〔kən'kluʒən〕*n.* 結論

in conclusion 總之   **not…at all** 一點也不…

fun〔fʌn〕*adj.* 好玩的；有趣的

terrifying〔'tɛrə,faɪɪŋ〕*adj.* 可怕的

experience〔ɪk'spɪrɪəns〕*n.* 經驗   stay〔ste〕*v.* 保持

calm〔kɑm〕*adj.* 冷靜的   **information desk** 服務台

police officer 警察   assistance〔ə'sɪstəns〕*n.* 幫助

lose one's **head** 慌張   wit〔wɪt〕*n.* 智慧

keep one's **wits about** one 保持冷靜；臨危不亂

smart〔smɑrt〕*adj.* 聰明的   way〔we〕*n.* 路

英語即席演講 ⑱

準備時間：5 分鐘

演講時間：2～3 分鐘

【資料來源：台北縣國民中小學英語競賽國中組】

Speech 18

Welcome, everyone.

It's a pleasure to have you here.

It's time to get things started.

Pets can be wonderful companions.

They can be cute, cuddly, and loyal.

But they are also a big responsibility.

Today, I'd like to tell a story about Tim.

Who is Tim?

Listen up, and I'll tell you all about him.

pleasure ('plɛʒɚ)
pet (pɛt)
companion (kəm'pænjən)
cuddly ('kʌdlɪ)
responsibility (rɪˌspɑnsə'bɪlətɪ)
listen up

get things started
wonderful ('wʌndɚfəl)
cute (kjut)
loyal ('lɔɪəl)

Tim had always wanted a pet.

He asked his mom if he could get one.

His mom agreed.

That afternoon, they went to the

   pet store.

There were many different pets there.

In the window, Tim saw a cute puppy.

"That's the dog I want," Tim said

   happily.

"I'll name him Spot!"

And with that, Tim took Spot home.

agree〔ə'gri〕	window〔'wɪndo〕
puppy〔'pʌpɪ〕	name〔nem〕
spot〔spɑt〕	***with that***

Tim spent a lot of time with Spot.

They seemed to always be together.

Spot grew to love Tim very much.

Tim fed Spot dog food.

Tim walked Spot every day.

Tim taught Spot how to do tricks.

Spot would bark when Tim came home.

He was always so happy to see Tim.

Tim and Spot were best friends.

seem (sim)

feed (fid)

trick (trɪk)

bark (bɑrk)

grow to + V.

walk (wɔk)

do tricks

As time passed, Tim started to
  ignore Spot.
Tim grew to like other things.
Tim spent less and less time with Spot.

Tim would be busy playing video games.
Tim would be out with his friends.
Sometimes, Tim would forget to feed
  Spot.

Spot started to feel lonely.
He no longer felt loved by Tim.
Their relationship had changed.

as〔əz, æz〕	pass〔pæs〕
as time passed	ignore〔ɪg'nor〕
be busy + V-ing	*video game*
sometimes〔'sʌm,taɪmz〕	
lonely〔'lonlɪ〕	*no longer*
relationship〔rɪ'leʃən,ʃɪp〕	change〔tʃendʒ〕

***One day*, *Tim came home from school*.**

But when he arrived, something was
  wrong.

He could not hear any barking.

"Spot?" cried Tim. "Where are you?"

There was no answer.

Tim realized that Spot had run away.

He looked around for many days.

But he never saw Spot again.

Tim felt great sorrow in his heart.

one day	wrong〔rɔŋ〕
cry〔kraɪ〕	answer〔'ænsɚ〕
realize〔'riə,laɪz〕	***run away***
look around	great〔gret〕
sorrow〔'sɑro〕	***in one's heart***

Having a pet is a special relationship.

We have to love and care for them always.

Like people, they have feelings.

Tim didn't value his relationship with Spot.

He had taken Spot for granted.

In the end, the relationship ended.

We can all learn from Tim's story.

We should always cherish our

　relationships.

Otherwise, we will feel nothing but regret!

have〔hæv〕

care for

value〔'væljʊ〕

take…for granted

cherish〔'tʃɛrɪʃ〕

nothing but

special〔'spɛʃəl〕

feelings〔'filɪŋz〕

grant〔grænt〕

in the end

otherwise〔'ʌðɚˌwaɪz〕

regret〔rɪ'grɛt〕

■ Speech 18

● 演講解說

Welcome**, **everyone.	歡迎大家。
It's a pleasure to have you here.	很高興你們能來這裡。
It's time to get things started.	該開始了。
Pets can be wonderful companions.	寵物可能是很棒的同伴。
They can be cute, cuddly,	牠們可能很可愛、令人想擁抱，
and loyal.	而且忠實。
But they are also a big responsibility.	但是牠們也是一個重責大任。
Today, I'd like to tell a story about	今天，我想說一個關於提姆的
Tim.	故事。
Who is Tim?	提姆是誰？
Listen up, and I'll tell you all about	注意聽，我要告訴你們關於他
him.	的事。

** ————————————————

pleasure〔ˈplɛʒɚ〕*n.* 高興的事　***get things started*** 開始（= *start*）

pet〔pɛt〕*n.* 寵物　wonderful〔ˈwʌndɚfəl〕*adj.* 很棒的

companion〔kəmˈpænjən〕*n.* 同伴　cute〔kjut〕*adj.* 可愛的

cuddly〔ˈkʌdlɪ〕*adj.* 令人想擁抱的　loyal〔ˈlɔɪəl〕*adj.* 忠實的

responsibility〔rɪˌspɑnsəˈbɪlətɪ〕*n.* 責任　***listen up*** 注意聽

Tim had always wanted a pet.　提姆一直想要一隻寵物。

He asked his mom if he could get one.　他問媽媽是否可以買一隻。

His mom agreed.　他媽媽同意了。

That afternoon, they went to the
　pet store.　那天下午，他們去寵物店。

There were many different pets there.　那裡有許多不同的寵物。

In the window, Tim saw a cute
　puppy.　提姆看到櫥窗裡有一隻可愛
的小狗。

"That's the dog I want," Tim said
　happily.　「那就是我想要的狗，」提姆
高興地說。

"I'll name him Spot!"　「我要給他取名為史巴特！」

And with that, Tim took Spot
　home.　於是，提姆就把史巴特帶回
家了。

**

agree〔ə'gri〕v. 同意

window〔'wɪndo〕n. 櫥窗　　puppy〔'pʌpɪ〕n. 小狗

name〔nem〕v. 替…取名　　spot〔spɑt〕n. 斑點

with that 於是；然後

Tim spent a lot of time with Spot.	提姆花很多時間陪史巴特。
They seemed to always be together.	他們似乎總是在一起。
Spot grew to love Tim very much.	史巴特漸漸喜歡上提姆。
Tim fed Spot dog food.	提姆會餵史巴特吃狗食。
Tim walked Spot every day.	提姆會每天帶史巴特去散步。
Tim taught Spot how to do tricks.	提姆會教史巴特表演把戲。
Spot would bark when Tim came home.	當提姆回到家時,史巴特會吠叫。
He was always so happy to see Tim.	看到提姆他總是很高興。
Tim and Spot were best friends.	提姆和史巴特是最好的朋友。

** ──────────────────

seem〔sim〕*v.* 似乎　　***grow to + V.*** 變得～

feed〔fid〕*v.* 餵【三態變化爲:feed-fed〔fɛd〕-fed】

walk〔wɔk〕*v.* 遛(狗)

trick〔trɪk〕*n.* 把戲　　***do tricks*** 表演把戲

bark〔bɑrk〕*v.* 吠叫

As *time passed*, *Tim started to ignore*
    ***Spot*.**

Tim grew to like other things.

Tim spent less and less time with
    Spot.

隨著時間的過去，提姆開始
忽視史巴特。

提姆漸漸喜歡上別的東西。

提姆陪史巴特的時間越來
越少。

Tim would be busy playing video
    games.

Tim would be out with his friends.

Sometimes, Tim would forget to
    feed Spot.

提姆會忙著打電動。

提姆會和他的朋友出去。

有時候，提姆會忘記餵史
巴特。

Spot started to feel lonely.

He no longer felt loved by Tim.

Their relationship had changed.

史巴特開始感到寂寞。

他再也感受不到提姆的愛。

他們的關係改變了。

＊＊ ──────────────────

as〔əz , æz〕*conj.* 隨著   pass〔pæs〕*v.* 過去

as time passed 隨著時間的過去   ignore〔ɪg'nor〕*v.* 忽視

be busy + V-ing 忙於～   *video game* 電動遊戲

sometimes〔'sʌm,taɪmz〕*adv.* 有時候

lonely〔'lonlɪ〕*adj.* 寂寞的   *no longer* 不再

relationship〔rɪ'leʃən,ʃɪp〕*n.* 關係

change〔tʃendʒ〕*v.* 改變

One day**, **Tim came home from school.	有一天，提姆放學回到家。
But when he arrived, something was wrong.	但是當他到家時，有點不太對勁。
He could not hear any barking.	他聽不到任何吠叫聲。
"Spot?" cried Tim. "Where are you?"	「史巴特？」提姆大叫。 「你在哪裡？」
There was no answer.	沒有回答。
Tim realized that Spot had run away.	提姆知道史巴特跑走了。
He looked around for many days.	他到處找了很多天。
But he never saw Spot again.	但是他再也不曾看過史巴特。
Tim felt great sorrow in his heart.	提姆的心裡感到很傷心。

✽✽ ————————————————————

one day 有一天 wrong〔rɔŋ〕*adj.* 不對勁的
cry〔kraɪ〕*v.* 大叫 answer〔'ænsɚ〕*n.* 回答
realize〔'riə͵laɪz〕*v.* 了解；知道 ***run away*** 逃跑
look around 環顧四周；到處去看
great〔gret〕*adj.* 很大的 sorrow〔'sɑro〕*n.* 悲傷
in** one's **heart 在內心深處

Having a pet is a special relationship.

We have to love and care for them
 always.

Like people, they have feelings.

養寵物是一種很特別的關係。

我們必須永遠愛惜並照顧
牠們。

牠們像人一樣，是有感情的。

Tim didn't value his relationship
 with Spot.

He had taken Spot for granted.

In the end, the relationship ended.

提姆不重視和史巴特之間的
關係。

他認為史巴特不需要特別關注。

到最後，這段關係就結束了。

We can all learn from Tim's story.

We should always cherish our
 relationships.

Otherwise, we will feel nothing but
 regret!

我們都可以從提姆的故事中學習。

我們應該永遠珍惜我們跟別人
之間的關係。

否則，我們只會感到後悔！

** ————————————————————

have〔hæv〕*v.* 飼養　special〔'spɛʃəl〕*adj.* 特別的

care for 照顧　feelings〔'filɪŋz〕*n. pl.* 感情

value〔'væljʊ〕*v.* 重視　grant〔grænt〕*v.* 給予；答應

take…for granted 把…視為理所當然；不把…當成特別需要
 注意的人或物

in the end 最後；結果　cherish〔'tʃɛrɪʃ〕*v.* 珍惜

otherwise〔'ʌðɚ͵waɪz〕*adv.* 否則

nothing but 只不過；僅僅　regret〔rɪ'grɛt〕*n.* 後悔

英語即席演講 ⑲

準備時間：5 分鐘

演講時間：2～3 分鐘

【資料來源：台北縣國民中小學英語競賽國中組】

Speech 19

Ladies and gentlemen, listen up.

I'd like to begin by welcoming you here.

It's a pleasure to see all of you.

Do you have a sweet tooth?

I sure do.

Sweet food sure is yummy.

However, we have to watch out.

Too many sweets can be very bad for us.

Let me tell you about a boy named Peter.

listen up	pleasure (ˋplɛʒɚ)
sweet (swit)	tooth (tuθ)
have a sweet tooth	sure (ʃur)
yummy (ˋjʌmɪ)	*watch out*
sweets (swits)	*named* ~

Peter was a boy who loved to eat sweets.

It seemed like he was addicted to them.

He ate sweets at every meal.

He would eat cake for breakfast.

He would eat ice cream for lunch.

He would drink soda at dinner.

Peter also didn't like to brush his teeth.

Actually, he was very lazy about it.

It wasn't long before Peter ran into

   trouble.

seem (sim)

be addicted to

soda ('sodə)

teeth (tiθ)

lazy ('lezɪ)

run into

addict (ə'dɪkt)

meal (mil)

brush (brʌʃ)

actually ('æktʃuəlɪ)

It wasn't long before ~

trouble ('trʌbl̩)

One day, Peter felt a sharp pain.

It came from his mouth.

Peter had a bad toothache.

He used his finger to wiggle his tooth.

"Ouch!" shouted Peter.

"That really hurts!"

Peter tried to ignore it as best he could.

But in the end, it hurt far too much.

Peter had to do something.

---

one day	sharp〔ʃɑrp〕
pain〔pen〕	mouth〔maʊθ〕
bad〔bæd〕	toothache〔'tuθ,ek〕
finger〔'fɪŋgɚ〕	wiggle〔'wɪgl̩〕
ouch〔aʊtʃ〕	shout〔ʃaʊt〕
hurt〔hɝt〕	***try to + V.***
ignore〔ɪg'nor〕	***as best one can***
in the end	far〔fɑr〕

Peter decided to see the dentist, Dr. Molar.

Dr. Molar looked at Peter's teeth.

Peter's teeth were in bad shape.

Peter confessed his love for sweets.

He also said he hated brushing his teeth.

Dr. Molar was very concerned.

"*You* eat too many sweets," said Dr.

  Molar.

"*You* also don't take care of your teeth."

"If you don't smarten up, I'll have to

  pull them all out!"

---

decide (dɪˈsaɪd)

shape (ʃep)

confess (kənˈfɛs)

concerned (kənˈsɝnd)

smarten (ˈsmɑrtn̩)

pull out

dentist (ˈdɛntɪst)

in bad shape

hate (het)

take care of

pull (pʊl)

***From then on*, *Peter was different*.**

He was scared by what the dentist said.

Peter was a changed boy.

He started brushing his teeth regularly.

He brushed them morning, noon,

and night.

He even began to use dental floss.

Peter also cut down on the sweets he ate.

Dr. Molar was proud of Peter.

Peter was glad he got to keep his teeth!

from then on	different (ˈdɪfrənt)
scare (skɛr)	changed (tʃendʒd)
regularly (ˈrɛgjələ·lɪ)	noon (nun)
dental (ˈdɛntḷ)	floss (flɔs)
cut down on	proud (praʊd)
be proud of	glad (glæd)
get to	keep (kip)

Sweets can be a nice treat once in a while.

But we also need to be careful

  with them.

Like anything, too many are not good.

We also need to have good oral hygiene.

Remember to brush after every meal.

Get regular checkups from the dentist.

Your teeth are very important.

Be sure to take good care of them.

Your beautiful smile depends on it!

---

treat〔trit〕	*once in a while*
careful〔'kɛrfəl〕	oral〔'orəl〕
hygiene〔'haɪdʒin〕	regular〔'rɛgjələ〕
checkup〔'tʃɛkˌʌp〕	important〔ɪm'pɔrtn̩t〕
be sure to + V.	*depend on*

■ Speech 19

● 演講解說

Ladies and gentlemen, listen up.	各位先生、各位女士,注意聽。
I'd like to begin by welcoming you here.	我一開始想要先歡迎你們來到這裡。
It's a pleasure to see all of you.	很高興看到你們。
Do you have a sweet tooth?	你們喜歡吃甜食嗎?
I sure do.	我當然喜歡吃。
Sweet food sure is yummy.	甜食的確很好吃。
However, we have to watch out.	然而,我們必須注意。
Too many sweets can be very bad for us.	太多甜食可能會對我們有害。
Let me tell you about a boy named Peter.	讓我告訴你們一個名叫彼得的男孩的事。

**

listen up 注意聽　　pleasure〔ˈplɛʒɚ〕*n.* 高興的事

sweet〔swit〕*adj.* 甜的　　tooth〔tuθ〕*n.* 牙齒;愛好

have a sweet tooth 嗜吃甜食　　sure〔ʃʊr〕*adv.* 當然;的確

yummy〔ˈjʌmɪ〕*adj.* 好吃的　　*watch out* 注意

sweets〔swits〕*n. pl.* 甜食　　*named*~ 名叫~

Peter was a boy who loved to eat sweets.	彼得是一個愛吃甜食的男孩。
It seemed like he was addicted to them.	看起來像是他對甜食上癮了。
He ate sweets at every meal.	他每餐都吃甜食。
He would eat cake for breakfast.	他早餐會吃蛋糕。
He would eat ice cream for lunch.	他午餐會吃冰淇淋。
He would drink soda at dinner.	他會在晚餐時喝汽水。
Peter also didn't like to brush his teeth.	彼得也不喜歡刷牙。
Actually, he was very lazy about it.	事實上，他是很懶得刷。
It wasn't long before Peter ran into trouble.	不久後，彼得就碰上麻煩了。

** ────────────

seem〔sim〕*v.* 似乎；看起來

addict〔ə'dɪkt〕*v.* 使上癮   ***be addicted to*** 對…上癮

meal〔mil〕*n.* 一餐   soda〔'sodə〕*n.* 汽水

brush〔brʌʃ〕*v.* 刷   teeth〔tiθ〕*n. pl.* 牙齒

actually〔'æktʃʊəlɪ〕*adv.* 事實上

lazy〔'lezɪ〕*adj.* 懶惰的

It wasn't long before ～ 不久後就～

run into 遭遇；陷入   trouble〔'trʌbl̩〕*n.* 麻煩

One day, *Peter felt a sharp pain*.	有一天，彼得感到劇烈的疼痛。
It came from his mouth.	疼痛來自他的嘴巴。
Peter had a bad toothache.	彼得牙齒很痛。
He used his finger to wiggle his tooth.	他用手指去搖動他的牙齒。
"Ouch!" shouted Peter.	「哎喲！」彼得大叫。
"That really hurts!"	「真痛！」
Peter tried to ignore it as best he could.	彼得想要盡力忽略疼痛。
But in the end, it hurt far too much.	但是最後，它實在太痛了。
Peter had to do something.	彼得必須想點辦法。

** ————————————————————

one day 有一天　　sharp〔ʃɑrp〕*adj.* 劇烈的

pain〔pen〕*n.* 疼痛　　mouth〔mauθ〕*n.* 嘴巴

bad〔bæd〕*adj.* 嚴重的　　toothache〔'tuθˌek〕*n.* 牙痛

finger〔'fɪŋɚ〕*n.* 手指　　wiggle〔'wɪgḷ〕*v.* 搖動

ouch〔autʃ〕*interj.* 哎喲　　shout〔ʃaut〕*v.* 喊叫

hurt〔hɝt〕*v.* 痛　　*try to* + *V.* 想要～

ignore〔ɪg'nor〕*v.* 忽視　　*as best one can* 盡力

in the end 最後　　far〔fɑr〕*adv.* 大大地

Peter decided to see the dentist, Dr. Molar.	彼得決定去看牙醫，莫勒醫生。
Dr. Molar looked at Peter's teeth.	莫勒醫生檢查彼得的牙齒。
Peter's teeth were in bad shape.	彼得的牙齒狀況很差。
Peter confessed his love for sweets.	彼得坦承自己愛吃甜食。
He also said he hated brushing his teeth.	他也說他討厭刷牙。
Dr. Molar was very concerned.	莫勒醫生非常擔心。
"You eat too many sweets," said Dr. Molar.	「你吃太多甜食了，」莫勒醫生說。
"You also don't take care of your teeth."	「你也不照顧自己的牙齒。」
"If you don't smarten up, I'll have to pull them all out!"	「如果你不聰明點，我就不得不把它們全部都拔掉！」

** ——————————

decide〔dɪ'saɪd〕*v.* 決定　　dentist〔'dɛntɪst〕*n.* 牙醫

shape〔ʃep〕*n.* 狀況　　*in bad shape* 處於不佳狀況

confess〔kən'fɛs〕*v.* 坦承　　hate〔het〕*v.* 討厭

concerned〔kən'sɝnd〕*adj.* 擔心的　　*take care of* 照顧

smarten〔'smɑrtn̩〕*v.* 變得更聰明 < *up* >

pull〔pʊl〕*v.* 拉　　*pull out* 拉出；拔出

***From then on**, Peter was different*.	從那時起，彼得不一樣了。
He was scared by what the dentist said.	他被牙醫所說的話嚇到了。
Peter was a changed boy.	彼得判若兩人。
He started brushing his teeth regularly.	他開始定期刷牙。
He brushed them morning, noon, and night.	他在早上、中午和晚上刷牙。
He even began to use dental floss.	他甚至開始使用牙線。
Peter also cut down on the sweets he ate.	彼得也減少吃甜食的量。
Dr. Molar was proud of Peter.	莫勒醫生以彼得為榮。
Peter was glad he got to keep his teeth!	彼得很高興他能保住牙齒！

** ——————————————————

from then on 從那時起   different〔'dɪfrənt〕*adj.* 不同的

scare〔skɛr〕*v.* 使驚嚇   changed〔tʃendʒd〕*adj.* 不同以往的

regularly〔'rɛgjələ⋅lɪ〕*adv.* 定期地；有規律地

noon〔nun〕*n.* 中午   dental〔'dɛntḷ〕*adj.* 牙齒的

floss〔flɔs〕*n.* 牙線   ***cut down on*** 減少（食品、香煙等的）量

proud〔praʊd〕*adj.* 驕傲的；感到光榮的

be proud of 以～為榮   glad〔glæd〕*adj.* 高興的

get to 得以；能夠   keep〔kip〕*v.* 保有

Sweets can be a nice treat once in a while.   甜食有時候可以是很好的
                                                  東西。

But we also need to be careful with them.   但是我們也必須小心它們。

Like anything, too many are not good.   就像任何其他東西一樣，太多
                                                   就不好了。

We also need to have good oral hygiene.   我們也需要有好的口腔衛生。

Remember to brush after every meal.   要記得飯後刷牙。

Get regular checkups from the dentist.   要定期請牙醫檢查。

Your teeth are very important.   你的牙齒很重要。

Be sure to take good care of them.   一定要好好照顧它們。

Your beautiful smile depends on it!   你美麗的笑容就靠它了！

**

treat〔trit〕*n.* 非常好的事物

once in a while 偶爾；有時候

careful〔'kɛrfəl〕*adj.* 小心的

oral〔'orəl〕*adj.* 口部的　　hygiene〔'haɪdʒin〕*n.* 衛生

regular〔'rɛgjələ·〕*adj.* 定期的　　checkup〔'tʃɛk͵ʌp〕*n.* 檢查

important〔ɪm'pɔrtn̩t〕*adj.* 重要的

be sure to + V. 一定要…　　*depend on* 依賴；依靠

英語即席演講 ⑳

準備時間：5 分鐘

演講時間：2～3 分鐘

【資料來源：台北縣國民中小學英語競賽國中組】

Speech 20

Good day to you all.
I welcome you.
Let's get started.

What do you like to do for fun?
What do you do in your spare time?
Did you know that it can affect your
    health?

Well today, I'm going to tell you a story.
It's a story about two siblings.
It's a story about Jack and Jill.

---

good day	***get started***
for fun	spare (spɛr)
spare time	affect (ə'fɛkt)
health (hɛlθ)	well (wɛl)
sibling ('sɪblɪŋ)	

Jack and Jill were brother and sister.

They liked keeping each other company.

They enjoyed all sorts of indoor
   activities.

Jack loved watching television best.

He watched comedies and dramas.

He watched movies the most.

Jill preferred playing on the computer.

She played all the latest games.

She surfed the Internet until late at night.

---

company (ˈkʌmpənɪ)   *keep sb. company*

enjoy (ɪnˈdʒɔɪ)   sort (sɔrt)

indoor (ˈɪnˌdor)   activity (ækˈtɪvətɪ)

comedy (ˈkɑmədɪ)   drama (ˈdrɑmə)

prefer (prɪˈfɝ)   computer (kəmˈpjutɚ)

latest (ˈletɪst)   surf (sɝf)

Internet (ˈɪntɚˌnɛt)   *surf the Internet*

late (let)   *late at night*

However, Jack and Jill never went

outside.

They spent all of their free time indoors.

Slowly, their bodies started to change.

Jack started to gain a lot of weight.

He was feeling sluggish all the time.

His tummy was getting bigger and bigger.

Jill's vision started getting worse.

Her eyes were always sore and tired.

Things looked very blurry to Jill.

outside ('aʊt'saɪd)

indoors ('ɪn'dorz)

gain (gen)

gain weight

all the time

vision ('vɪʒən)

sore (sor)

blurry ('blɝɪ)

free time

slowly ('sloli)

weight (wet)

sluggish ('slʌgɪʃ)

tummy ('tʌmɪ)

worse (wɝs)

tired (taɪrd)

Jack and Jill went to see the doctor.

The doctor took some x-rays of Jack.

The doctor also tested Jill's eyesight.

Jack wasn't as healthy as he used to be.

He was always sitting in front
  of the TV.

Jack wasn't moving around enough.

Jill's vision was worsening.

She could hardly read the eye chart.

Jill was not giving her eyes enough rest.

take (tek)	x-ray ('ɛks're)
test (tɛst)	eyesight ('aɪ,saɪt)
healthy ('hɛlθɪ)	***used to*** + *V*.
in front of	***move around***
worsen ('wɝsn̩)	hardly ('hardlɪ)
read (rid)	chart (tʃart)
eye chart	rest (rɛst)

After that, **they changed their hobbies**.

They decided to be more active.

They began to enjoy the outdoors.

They started riding bicycles.

They started playing in the park.

They even tried some rollerblading.

Jack got thinner.

Jill's vision improved.

Both of them felt better and had

more fun!

change〔tʃendʒ〕	hobby〔'hɑbɪ〕
decide〔dɪ'saɪd〕	active〔'æktɪv〕
outdoors〔'aʊt'dorz〕	ride〔raɪd〕
bicycle〔'baɪsɪkl̩〕	
rollerblading〔'rolɚˌbledɪŋ〕	thin〔θɪn〕
improve〔ɪm'pruv〕	**have fun**

There are many fun outdoor activities.

We shouldn't stay inside all the time.

Being outdoors can improve

   our health.

Try hiking in the mountains.

Go swimming with some friends.

Take the dog for a walk.

Don't always be stuck indoors.

Go out and get some fresh air.

An active lifestyle is a healthy one!

fun〔fʌn〕	outdoor〔'aʊtˌdor〕
stay〔ste〕	inside〔'ɪn'saɪd〕
hike〔haɪk〕	***in the mountains***
take ~ for a walk	stick〔stɪk〕
fresh〔frɛʃ〕	air〔ɛr〕
lifestyle〔'laɪfˌstaɪl〕	healthy〔'hɛlθɪ〕

■ Speech 20

● 演講解說

Good day to you all.	大家好。
I welcome you.	歡迎你們。
Let's get started.	我們開始吧。
What do you like to do for fun?	你喜歡做些什麼好玩的事？
What do you do in your spare time?	你空閒時間都做些什麼？
Did you know that it can affect your health?	你知道這可能會影響你的健康嗎？
Well today, I'm going to tell you a story.	那麼今天，我要告訴你們一個故事。
It's a story about two siblings.	它是一個關於一對兄妹的故事。
It's a story about Jack and Jill.	它是一個關於傑克和吉兒的故事。

**

good day 日安；您好   ***get started*** 開始
for fun 為了樂趣   spare〔spɛr〕*adj.* 空閒的
spare time 空閒時間   affect〔əˋfɛkt〕*v.* 影響
health〔hɛlθ〕*n.* 健康   well〔wɛl〕*interj.* 嗯
sibling〔ˋsɪblɪŋ〕*n.* (不分男女的) 兄弟姊妹

Jack and Jill were brother and sister.

傑克和吉兒是兄妹。

They liked keeping each other company.

他們喜歡互相作伴。

They enjoyed all sorts of indoor
   activities.

他們喜歡各式各樣的室內
活動。

Jack loved watching television best.

傑克最愛看電視。

He watched comedies and dramas.

他會看喜劇和戲劇。

He watched movies the most.

他電影看得最多。

Jill preferred playing on the computer.

吉兒比較喜歡打電腦。

She played all the latest games.

她會玩所有最新的遊戲。

She surfed the Internet until late
   at night.

她會上網上到深夜。

** ————————————————

company〔'kʌmpənɪ〕*n.* 同伴

keep** sb. **company 與某人作伴

enjoy〔ɪn'dʒɔɪ〕*v.* 喜歡   sort〔sɔrt〕*n.* 種類

indoor〔'ɪnˌdor〕*adj.* 室內的   activity〔æk'tɪvətɪ〕*n.* 活動

comedy〔'kɑmədɪ〕*n.* 喜劇   drama〔'drɑmə〕*n.* 戲劇

prefer〔prɪ'fɝ〕*v.* 比較喜歡   computer〔kəm'pjutɚ〕*n.* 電腦

latest〔'letɪst〕*adj.* 最新的   surf〔sɝf〕*v.* 衝浪

Internet〔'ɪntɚˌnɛt〕*n.* 網際網路   ***surf the Internet*** 上網

late〔let〕*adv.* 到很晚;到深夜   ***late at night*** 在深夜

However, *Jack and Jill never went* | 然而，傑克與吉兒從不外
outside. | 出。
They spent all of their free time | 他們在室內度過所有的空閒
  indoors. | 時間。
Slowly, their bodies started to | 慢慢地，他們的身體開始有
  change. | 了變化。

Jack started to gain a lot of weight. | 傑克的體重開始直線上升。
He was feeling sluggish all the time. | 他一直覺得懶洋洋的。
His tummy was getting bigger and | 他的肚子變得越來越大。
  bigger. |

Jill's vision started getting worse. | 吉兒的視力開始變差。
Her eyes were always sore and tired. | 她的眼睛總是又痛又累。
Things looked very blurry to Jill. | 對吉兒來說，每樣東西看起
  | 來都很模糊。

** ——————————————————

outside〔'aʊt'saɪd〕*adv.* 到戶外　　*free time* 空閒時間

indoors〔'ɪn'dorz〕*adv.* 在室內　　slowly〔'sloli〕*adv.* 慢慢地

gain〔gen〕*v.* 獲得；增加　　weight〔wet〕*n.* 重量；體重

gain weight 增加體重

sluggish〔'slʌgɪʃ〕*adj.* 缺乏活力的；懶洋洋的

all the time 一直　　tummy〔'tʌmɪ〕*n.* 肚子

vision〔'vɪʒən〕*n.* 視力　　worse〔wɜs〕*adj.* 更差的

sore〔sor〕*adj.* 疼痛的　　tired〔taɪrd〕*adj.* 疲倦的；累的

blurry〔'blɜɪ〕*adj.* 模糊不清的

Jack and Jill went to see the doctor.   傑克和吉兒去看醫生。

The doctor took some x-rays of Jack.   醫生為傑克拍了幾張 X 光片。

The doctor also tested Jill's eyesight.   醫生也檢查了吉兒的視力。

Jack wasn't as healthy as he used to be.   傑克不像以前那麼健康。

He was always sitting in front of the TV.   他總是坐在電視機前。

Jack wasn't moving around enough.   傑克沒有充分地走動。

Jill's vision was worsening.   吉兒的視力在惡化。

She could hardly read the eye chart.   她幾乎看不清視力檢查表。

Jill was not giving her eyes enough rest.   吉兒沒有讓眼睛充分休息。

** ─────────────────

take〔tek〕*v.* 拍攝　　x-ray〔'ɛks,re〕*n.* X 光片

test〔tɛst〕*v.* 檢查　　eyesight〔'aɪ,saɪt〕*n.* 視力

healthy〔'hɛlθɪ〕*adj.* 健康的　　***used to + V.*** 以前…

in front of 在…前面　　***move around*** 走來走去

worsen〔'wɝsn̩〕*v.* 惡化

hardly〔'hardlɪ〕*adv.* 幾乎不

read〔rid〕*v.* 判讀　　chart〔tʃart〕*n.* 圖表

eye chart 視力檢查表　　rest〔rɛst〕*n.* 休息

After that, *they changed their*
    hobbies.

在那之後，他們改變了嗜好。

They decided to be more active.

他們決定要多活動。

They began to enjoy the outdoors.

他們開始享受戶外活動。

They started riding bicycles.

他們開始騎腳踏車。

They started playing in the park.

他們開始去公園玩。

They even tried some rollerblading.

他們甚至嘗試溜一下直排輪。

Jack got thinner.

傑克變瘦了。

Jill's vision improved.

吉兒的視力也改善了。

Both of them felt better and had
    more fun!

他們兩人都覺得好多了，並
且玩得更愉快！

**   ————————————————

change〔tʃendʒ〕*v.* 改變   hobby〔'hɑbɪ〕*n.* 嗜好

decide〔dɪ'saɪd〕*v.* 決定

active〔'æktɪv〕*adj.* 活動的；活躍的

outdoors〔'aʊt'dorz〕*n.* 野外活動   *adv.* 向戶外

ride〔raɪd〕*v.* 騎   bicycle〔'baɪsɪkl̩〕*n.* 腳踏車

rollerblading〔'rolɚ‚bledɪŋ〕*n.* 直排輪溜冰鞋運動

thin〔θɪn〕*adj.* 瘦的   improve〔ɪm'pruv〕*v.* 改善

have fun 玩得愉快

There are many fun outdoor activities.	有許多有趣的戶外活動。
We shouldn't stay inside all the time.	我們不應該一直待在室內。
Being outdoors can improve our health.	到戶外能改善我們的健康。
Try hiking in the mountains.	試著去山裡健行。
Go swimming with some friends.	跟一些朋友去游泳。
Take the dog for a walk.	帶狗去散步。
Don't always be stuck indoors.	不要老是待在室內。
Go out and get some fresh air.	出去呼吸一些新鮮空氣。
An active lifestyle is a healthy one!	活躍的生活方式就是健康的生活方式！

** ————————————————

fun〔fʌn〕*adj.* 有趣的
outdoor〔'aʊtˌdor〕*adj.* 戶外的
stay〔ste〕*v.* 停留　　inside〔'ɪn'saɪd〕*adv.* 在室內
hike〔haɪk〕*v.* 健行　　*in the mountains* 在山區
take ~ for a walk 帶～去散步
stick〔stɪk〕*v.* 使停留；使困住
fresh〔frɛʃ〕*adj.* 新鮮的　　air〔ɛr〕*n.* 空氣
lifestyle〔'laɪfˌstaɪl〕*n.* 生活方式
healthy〔'hɛlθɪ〕*adj.* 健康的

臺北市 高級中學 高、國中 學生英語演講比賽實施要點

一、目　　的：為提昇高、國中學生英文程度，增進學生英語表達能力。

二、主辦單位：臺北市政府教育局

三、承辦單位：臺北市立景美女子高級中學

四、比賽時間：每年 11 月

五、比賽地點：臺北市立景美女子高級中學（電話：2936-8847 轉 207
傳真：2937-6801 地址：臺北市文山區木新路三段 312 號）

六、參加資格：

(一) 高中組：

1. 甲組：本市公、私立高級中學或職業學校修讀綜合高中學術學程或大陸地區臺商子女學校在學學生，未具乙組參賽條件之一者，每校得遴選一名參加。

2. 乙組：本市公、私立高級中學或職業學校修讀綜合高中學術學程或大陸地區臺商子女學校在學學生，具下列條件之一者，每校得遴選一名參加。

⑴國小三年級（含）以後，曾在國外英語地區或國內外僑學校雙語部就讀英語累計二年以上者。

⑵外國來華留學學生。

⑶曾參加教育部舉辦之全國高中學生英語演講比賽獲得全國前 3 名者，或曾獲得本市本項比賽第 1 名者。

⑷已參加本學年度高級中學英文作文比賽者。

(二) 國中組：

1. 甲組：本市公、私立國民中學或大陸地區臺商子女學校，未具乙組參賽條件之一者，每校遴選在學學生一名參加，先分二區辦理初賽，再辦理決賽。(第一區：大安、文山、松山、信義、南港、內湖等行政區。第二區：中正、萬華、大同、中山、士林、北投等行政區。大陸地區臺商子女學校，列入第一區及第二區等兩區中報名人數較少之部分與賽)

2. 乙組：本市公、私立國民中學或大陸地區臺商子女學校，具下列條件之一者，每校得遴選在學學生一名參加。

⑴國小一年級（含）以後，曾在國外英語地區或國內外僑學校、雙語部就讀英語累計二年以上者。

⑵外國來華留學學生。

⑶曾參加本市本項比賽獲得第 1 名者。

七、演講題目及演講時間：

(一) 高中組：

1. 演講題目：⑴ 指定題（參賽學生不得使用輔助圖片或道具）

⑵ 看圖即席演講：由臺北市政府教育局聘請命題委員命擬，於比賽當場抽籤決定，準備時間5分鐘。

2. 演講時間：⑴ 指定題：4分鐘。　⑵ 看圖即席演講：2分鐘。

(二) 國中組：

1. 演講題目：⑴ 指定題（參賽學生不得使用輔助圖片或道具）

⑵ 看圖即席演講：由臺北市政府教育局聘請命題委員命擬，於比賽當場抽籤決定，準備時間20分鐘。

2. 演講時間：⑴ 指定題：3分鐘。　⑵ 看圖即席演講：2分鐘。

※ 國中甲組分兩區（第一區、第二區），同時進行指定題演講與看圖即席演講比賽，總成績評定結果，第一區、第二區兩組各遴參賽人數的前25%（無條件進入）參加當天下午總決賽，採看圖即席演講方式。

※ 國中乙組則於上午直接進行決賽。

八、評分標準：

(一) 指定題演講與看圖即席演講各以一百分為滿分。並以指定題演講佔總成績40%，看圖即席演講佔總成績60%核計總成績。

(二) 指定題演講與看圖即席演講之評分標準均為：

1. 內容：佔40%　2. 語言表達能力（表達技巧、語言使用流暢度）：佔40%
3. 儀態：佔20%

(三) 國中甲組以決賽成績為最後的成績。

(四) 總成績遇有同分情形時，以看圖即席演講獲分較高者為優勝，並請評審委員另行討論決定。

九、獎　勵：

(一) 名額：

1. 高中各組：錄取第1名1人，第2名3人，第3名6人，頒發獎狀、獎品以資鼓勵。

2. 國中各組：錄取第1名1人，第2名3人，第3名4人，第4名5人，第5名若干人，頒發獎狀、獎品以資鼓勵。

(二) 以上錄取獎勵人數得視參加人數及成績，由評審委員酌予增減之。

(三) 獲得第1名之指導老師，予以敘小功乙次；第2名予以敘嘉獎兩次、第3名之指導老師，予以敘嘉獎乙次。（指導老師若指導兩位以上之學生，取其最優敘獎之，不重覆敘獎）

十、參賽學生一律穿著合宜之便服參加比賽，並請務必攜帶學生證，以備核驗。

十一、報名學生經查資格不符者，或其他違規情形者，取消參賽權；若已得獎者，取消得獎資格，並追回獎狀、獎品。